William Shakespeare

Shakespeare's Comedy of Measure for Measure

William Shakespeare

Shakespeare's Comedy of Measure for Measure

ISBN/EAN: 9783744788519

Printed in Europe, USA, Canada, Australia, Japan

Cover: Foto ©Andreas Hilbeck / pixelio.de

More available books at **www.hansebooks.com**

SHAKESPEARE'S

COMEDY OF

MEASURE FOR MEASURE.

EDITED, WITH NOTES,

BY

WILLIAM J. ROLFE, A.M.,

FORMERLY HEAD MASTER OF THE HIGH SCHOOL, CAMBRIDGE, MASS.

WITH ENGRAVINGS.

NEW YORK:

HARPER & BROTHERS, PUBLISHERS,

FRANKLIN SQUARE.

1884.

ENGLISH CLASSICS.

EDITED BY WM. J. ROLFE, A.M.

Illustrated. 16mo, Cloth, 56 cents per volume ; Paper, 40 cents per volume.

SHAKESPEARE'S WORKS.

The Merchant of Venice.	The Taming of the Shrew.
Othello.	All 's Well that Ends Well.
Julius Cæsar.	Coriolanus.
A Midsummer-Night's Dream.	The Comedy of Errors.
Macbeth.	Cymbeline.
Hamlet.	Antony and Cleopatra.
Much Ado about Nothing.	Measure for Measure.
Romeo and Juliet.	Merry Wives of Windsor.
As You Like It.	Love's Labour 's Lost.
The Tempest.	Two Gentlemen of Verona.
Twelfth Night.	Timon of Athens.
The Winter's Tale.	Troilus and Cressida.
King John.	Henry VI. Part I.
Richard II.	Henry VI. Part II.
Henry IV. Part I.	Henry VI. Part III.
Henry IV. Part II.	Pericles, Prince of Tyre.
Henry V.	The Two Noble Kinsmen.
Richard III.	Venus and Adonis, Lucrece, etc.
Henry VIII.	Sonnets.
King Lear.	Titus Andronicus.

GOLDSMITH'S SELECT POEMS.
GRAY'S SELECT POEMS.

PUBLISHED BY HARPER & BROTHERS, NEW YORK.

☞ *Any of the above works will be sent by mail, postage prepaid, to any part of the United States, on receipt of the price.*

CONTENTS.

THE MOATED GRANGE.

INTRODUCTION

TO

MEASURE FOR MEASURE.

I. THE HISTORY OF THE PLAY.

Measure for Measure was first printed in the folio of 1623, where it occupies pages 61–84 in the division of "Comedies." It was not entered on the Stationers' Registers, and is not mentioned by Meres in 1598. No direct allusion to it in Shakespeare's time has been found, and we have nothing to

fix the date of its composition but the style and versification,
with some minor points of internal evidence. The critics,
however, have generally agreed that the play was written in
1603 or early in 1604.

Tyrwhitt and Malone conjectured that the following passages offer "a courtly apology for King James I.'s stately
and ungracious demeanour on his entry into England:"

> "I 'll privily away. I love the people,
> But do not love to stage me to their eyes.
> Though it do well, I do not relish well
> Their loud applause and aves vehement" (i. 1. 67 fol.).

> "The general, subject to a well-wish'd king,
> Quit their own part, and in obsequious fondness
> Crowd to his presence, where their untaught love
> Must needs appear offence" (ii. 4. 27 fol.).

Ward (*Hist. of Dram. Lit.* 1. 408) is "inclined to accept this
conjecture, the more so that there is something in the sentiment of these passages not ill according with the tendency
towards shrinking from an unnecessary publicity, which we
may fairly suppose to have been an element in the poet's
own character."

Malone also saw historical allusions in i. 2. 4: "Heaven
grant us its peace," etc.; and in i. 2. 77: "What with the
war, what with the sweat," etc. James had early announced
his intention of ending the war with Spain which was in
progress when he came to the throne, and peace was concluded in the autumn of 1604. The year before, as Capell
pointed out, the "sweating-sickness," or plague, had carried
off more than thirty thousand people in London, about one
fifth of the entire population of the city.

In the first speech of iv. 3, among the ten prisoners mentioned are four "stabbers" and duellists; and, according to
Wilson the historian, the "roaring boys, bravadoes, roysters,"
and like characters had become so disorderly in 1604 that

the "act of stabbing" (1 Jac. I. c. 8) was passed to restrain them.

Fleay (*Manual*, p. 46), by his metrical tests, confirms this assumed date of 1603. He says : "This play is the central one for the metre of the third period ; it has more lines with extra syllables before a pause in the middle of a line than any other. It is freer in rhythm than any play of the first and second periods."

Furnivall, in his classification of the plays (see our ed. of *A. Y. L.* p. 25), puts *Measure for Measure* among the plays of the poet's "third period" (1601–1608), and dates it in 1603. He includes it with *Julius Cæsar* and *Hamlet* in the "unfit - nature, or under - burden - failing group," which he makes the first subdivision of that period ; adding in explanation that "the prison-scene, where Claudio's nature fails under the burden of coming death, is the centre of the play."

Tieck, followed by Ulrici and some other critics, was led by the peculiarities of style and sentiment to regard *Measure for Measure* as one of the very latest of the plays ; but, as Verplanck remarks, "the drama, in those very characteristics on which the theory is founded, most resembles *Othello*, *Lear*, the revised *Hamlet*, and in general those tragedies known to have been written between 1602 and 1607 ; while, on the contrary, its tone and fancy are entirely dissimilar from the pastoral beauties of the *Winter's Tale*, with the sprightliness of its gayer scenes, or the spirit of cheerful enjoyment which breathes in the mountain scenes of *Cymbeline*, both of them known to belong to a later period than that of *Lear*." *

II. THE SOURCES OF THE PLOT.

"The story, like that of *Othello*, comes originally from a novel of Cinthio, the Italian novelist and tragic author. He

* Compare what Dowden says of the tone of the latest plays in *Shakspere: his Mind and Art*, p. 358 fol. (American ed.) and in the *Shakspere Primer*, p. 54 fol.

was a prolific relater of dark and bloody stories, which have
yet such an air of reality as to give the impression that he
drew his materials, like Scott, from domestic traditions or
legal records. Shakespeare had also the same plot in Whetstone's tragedy of *Promos* and *Cassandra* (1578), founded on
Cinthio's novel. But he owed very little to either predecessor but the outline of the story, and some slight hints or cas-
ual expressions. It is evident that, in such a case, a previ-
ous tragedy on the same subject, instead of lessening Shakespeare's claims to originality, greatly increases them, as it
imposed on him the new difficulty of avoiding many obvious
images and ideas which must arise to every writer handling
the same incidents. Nor was Whetstone an author of so
low a rank that he might be safely neglected in this respect,
and his materials used without injustice or plagiarism. On
the contrary, he was, though inflated and extravagant in
style, and deficient in the power of interesting or exciting
his readers, a writer of learning and talent. He followed
Cinthio very closely, in making the sister (the 'woful Cassandra' of his play, the Epitia of Cinthio, and the Isabella of
Shakespeare) yield to the governor's desires and her brother's pusillanimous sophistry — a degradation which Shakespeare has avoided by the introduction of Mariana, and the
very venial artifice of Isabella, which Coleridge censures, but
which is certainly, if a blemish at all, a very light one com-
pared with the intrinsic repulsiveness of making the heroine
the wife of the guilty governor, and the supplicant for his
life. The inferior characters of Whetstone are the same
only in their habits and occupations—the painting of their
character is Shakespeare's own as much as that of the nobler personages, and the high moral wisdom which overflows
in their dialogue. Isabella, as a character, is entirely his
own creation. . . .

   "The probability of the plot has been objected to, but certainly without any reason ; for it singularly happens that we

have historical evidence of the occurrence of three or four very similar crimes, in different ages and countries. One of these is the well-known story of Col. Kirke, in the reign of James II., half a century after Shakespeare's death ; another occurred in Holland, a century before his birth, under Charles the Bold, and has lately been related from the old chroniclers, with all their antique simplicity, by Barante, in his delightful *Histoire des Ducs de Bourgogne.* Another of these Angelo-like abuses of power is said to have taken place under one of the old Dukes of Ferrara, and this may have been the actual foundation of Cinthio's tale. Shakespeare, whether he was acquainted with the original or not (as his use of the book in *Othello* indicates that he was), had the story before him, as Whetstone, a few years after the publication of his play, trans-lated and published it himself—retaining, however, the names, and interweaving the thoughts of his own drama. It is con-tained in his *Heptameron of Civil Discourses* (1582), and has been reprinted in Collier's *Shakespeare's Library.* He has also accompanied his own tragedy with an analytical ar-gument, which will enable the reader to compare Shake-speare's management of the plot with that of his predecessor :

"'In the city of Julio (sometime under the dominion of Corvinus, King of Hungary and Bohemia), there was a law, that what man soever committed adultery should lose his head, and the woman offender should wear some disguised apparel during her life, to make her infamously noted. This severe law, by the favour of some merciful magistrate, be-came little regarded, until the time of Lord Promos' author-ity, who, convicting a young gentleman, named Andrugio, of incontinency, condemned both him and his minion to the ex-ecution of this statute. Andrugio had a very virtuous and beautiful gentlewoman to his sister, named Cassandra : Cas-sandra, to enlarge her brother's life, submitted an humble petition to the Lord Promos. Promos, regarding her good behaviour and fantasying her great beauty, was much de-

lighted with the sweet order of her talk, and, doing good that
evil might come thereof, for a time he reprieved her brother;
but, wicked man, turning his liking into unlawful lust, he set
down the spoil of her honour ransom for her brother's life.
Chaste Cassandra, abhorring both him and his suit, by no
persuasion would yield to this ransom. But, in fine, won
with the importunity of her brother (pleading for life), upon
these conditions she agreed to Promos—first, that he should
pardon her brother, and after marry her. Promos, as fearless in promise as careless in performance, with solemn vow
signed her conditions; but, worse than any infidel, his will
satisfied, he performed neither the one nor the other; for,
to keep his authority unspotted with favour, and to prevent
Cassandra's clamours, he commanded the gaoler secretly to
present Cassandra with her brother's head. The gaoler,
with the outcries of Andrugio, abhorring Promos' lewdness,
by the providence of God provided thus for his safety. He
presented Cassandra with a felon's head, newly executed,
who (being mangled, knew it not from her brother's, who by
the gaoler was set at liberty) was so aggrieved at this treach-
ery, that, at the point to kill herself, she spared that stroke
to be avenged of Promos; and devising a way, she concluded
to make her fortunes known unto the king. She (executing
this resolution) was so highly favoured of the king, that forth-
with he hasted to do justice on Promos; whose judgment
was to marry Cassandra, to repair her erased honour; which
done, for his heinous offence he should lose his head. This
marriage solemnized, Cassandra, tied in the greatest bonds
of affection to her husband, became an earnest suitor for his
life. The king (tendering the general benefit of the commonweal before her special case, although he favoured her
much) would not grant her suit. Andrugio (disguised among
the company), sorrowing the grief of his sister, betrayed his
safety and craved pardon. The king, to renown the virtues
of Cassandra, pardoned both him and Promos.'

"The more authentic history of the Angelo of the Nether-lands is recorded by several of the old Dutch and Flemish chroniclers of the reign of Charles le Téméraire, the last of the more than royal dukes who reigned in different rights over the several states of Flanders, Holland, and Burgundy. (See Barante's *Histoire des Ducs de la Maison de Valois*.) The Angelo was here a very brave and renowned knight, who was governor of Flushing ; and it was the wife of a state crimi-nal, confined on a charge of sedition, who is tempted to yield up her honour on condition of receiving from the governor an order to the gaoler to deliver her husband up to her. In the meanwhile, a prior order had been sent ; the husband was secretly beheaded ; and the wife received, on presenting her order, a chest containing the bloody corpse. Upon the duke's visiting his principality of Zealand, she appealed to him for justice. The governor confessed his guilt, and threw himself with confidence upon the duke's mercy, relying on his former services and favour. The duke commanded him to marry the widow, and endow her formally with all his wealth. She at first shrunk with horror from the alliance, but at last consented to the ceremony, on the prayers of her family, who thought their honour involved in it. When this was done, the governor returned to the duke, and informed him that the injured person was now satisfied. 'So am not I,' replied this far more rigid ruler than Shakespeare's kind-hearted, philosophical duke. He sent the guilty man to the same prison where his victim had died. A confessor was sent with him ; and after the last rites of religion, without further delay, the governor was beheaded. His new wife and her friends had hurried to the prison, and arrived there only to receive the bloody trunk in the same manner that she had received the remains of her first husband. Over-come with horror, she fainted, and never recovered.

"Had Shakespeare adopted this version of the story, it would have afforded him a canvas for many a scene of ter-

rific, perhaps of too horrible, truth. But this would have de-
manded the omission or entire degradation of Isabella's character—one so differing from every other of the many admirable portraits he has left us of female excellence, that its
loss would have been dearly purchased, even by scenes of
terror or pathos vying with those of the last acts of *Lear* or
Othello."*

III. CRITICAL COMMENTS ON THE PLAY.

[*From Schlegel's " Dramatic Literature."* †]

In *Measure for Measure* Shakspeare was compelled, by
the nature of the subject, to make his poetry more familiar
with criminal justice than is usual with him. All kinds of
proceedings connected with the subject, all sorts of active
or passive persons, pass in review before us: the hypocrit-
ical lord deputy, the compassionate provost, and the hard-
hearted hangman; a young man of quality who is to suffer for the seduction of his mistress before marriage, loose
wretches brought in by the police, nay, even a hardened
criminal, whom even the preparations for his execution cannot awaken out of his callousness. But yet, notwithstand-
ing this agitating truthfulness, how tender and mild is the
pervading tone of the picture! The piece takes improperly
its name from punishment; the true significance of the whole
is the triumph of mercy over strict justice; no man being
himself so free from errors as to be entitled to deal it out to
his equals. The most beautiful embellishment of the composition is the character of Isabella, who, on the point of taking the veil, is yet prevailed upon by sisterly affection to
tread again the perplexing ways of the world, while, amid
the general corruption, the heavenly purity of her mind is
not even stained with one unholy thought: in the humble

* From Verplanck's Introduction to *M. for M.*

† *Lectures on Dramatic Art and Literature,* by A. W. Schlegel; Black's
translation, revised by Morrison (London, 1846), p. 387 fol.

robes of the novice she is a very angel of light. When the
cold and stern Angelo, heretofore of unblemished reputation, whom the duke has commissioned, during his pretend-
ed absence, to restrain, by a rigid administration of the laws,
the excesses of dissolute immorality, is even himself tempted
by the virgin charms of Isabella, supplicating for the pardon
of her brother Claudio, condemned to death for a youthful
indiscretion; when at first, in timid and obscure language,
he insinuates, but at last impudently avouches, his readiness
to grant Claudio's life to the sacrifice of her honour ; when
Isabella repulses his offer with a noble scorn ; in her account
of the interview to her brother, when the latter at first ap-
plauds her conduct, but at length, overcome by the fear of
death, strives to persuade her to consent to dishonour—in
these masterly scenes, Shakspeare has sounded the depths
of the human heart. The interest here reposes altogether
on the represented action ; curiosity contributes nothing to
our delight, for the duke, in the disguise of a monk, is always present to watch over his dangerous representative, and
to avert every evil which could possibly be apprehended ;
we look to him with confidence for a happy result. The
duke acts the part of the monk naturally, even to deception ; he unites in his person the wisdom of the priest and
the prince. Only in his wisdom he is too fond of round-
about ways ; his vanity is flattered with acting invisibly like
an earthly providence ; he takes more pleasure in overhear-
ing his subjects than governing them in the customary way
of princes. As he ultimately extends a free pardon to all
the guilty, we do not see how his original purpose, in com-
mitting the execution of the laws to other hands, of restoring
their strictness, has in any wise been accomplished. The
poet might have had this irony in view, that of the number-
less slanders of the duke, told him by the petulant Lucio, in
ignorance of the person whom he is addressing, that at least
which regarded his singularities and whims was not wholly

D

without foundation. It is deserving of remark, that Shakspeare, amidst the rancour of religious parties, takes a delight in painting the condition of a monk, and always repre-
sents his influence as beneficial. We find in him none of
the black and knavish monks, which an enthusiasm for Prot-
estantism, rather than poetical inspiration, has suggested to
some of our modern poets. Shakspeare merely gives his
monks an inclination to busy themselves in the affairs of others, after renouncing the world for themselves ; with respect,
however, to pious frauds, he does not represent them as very
conscientious. Such are the parts acted by the monk in
Romeo and Juliet, and another in *Much Ado about Nothing*,
and even by the duke, whom, contrary to the well-known
proverb, the cowl seems really to make a monk.

[*From Mrs. Jameson's " Characteristics of Women." ***]

The character of Isabella, considered as a poetical delineation, is less mixed than that of Portia ; and the dissimilar-
ity between the two appears, at first view, so complete that
we can scarce believe that the same elements enter into the
composition of each. Yet so it is ; they are portrayed as
equally wise, gracious, virtuous, fair, and young ; we perceive
in both the same exalted principle and firmness of character ; the same depth of reflection and persuasive eloquence ;
the same self-denying generosity and capability of strong
affections ; and we must wonder at that marvellous power
by which qualities and endowments essentially and closely
allied are so combined and modified as to produce a result
altogether different. " O Nature ! O Shakspeare ! which of
ye drew from the other?"

Isabella is distinguished from Portia, and strongly indi-
vidualized by a certain moral grandeur, a saintly grace,
something of vestal dignity and purity, which render her less
attractive and more imposing ; she is "severe in youthful

* American ed. (Boston, 1857), p. 83 fol.

beauty," and inspires a reverence which would have placed her beyond the daring of one unholy wish or thought, except in such a man as Angelo—

> " O cunning enemy, that, to catch a saint,
> With saints dost bait thy hook!"

This impression of her character is conveyed from the very first, when Lucio, the libertine jester, whose coarse audacious wit checks at every feather, thus expresses his respect for her :

> " I would not—though 't is my familiar sin
> With maids to seem the lapwing, and to jest
> Tongue far from heart—play with all virgins so.
> I hold you as a thing enskied and sainted;
> By your renouncement an immortal spirit,
> And to be talk'd with in sincerity,
> As with a saint."

A strong distinction between Isabella and Portia is produced by the circumstances in which they are respectively placed. Portia is a high-born heiress, "lord of a fair mansion, master of her servants, queen o'er herself;" easy and decided, as one born to command, and used to it. Isabella has also the innate dignity which renders her "queen o'er herself," but she has lived far from the world and its pomps and pleasures ; she is one of a consecrated sisterhood—a novice of St. Clare ; the power to command obedience and to confer happiness are to her unknown. Portia is a splendid creature, radiant with confidence, hope, and joy. She is like the orange-tree, hung at once with golden fruit and luxuriant flowers, which has expanded into bloom and fragrance beneath favouring skies, and has been nursed into beauty by the sunshine and the dews of heaven. Isabella is like a stately and graceful cedar, towering on some alpine cliff, unbowed and unscathed amid the storm. She gives us the impression of one who has passed under the ennobling discipline of suffering and self-denial : a melancholy charm tempers the natural vigour of her mind : her spirit seems to stand upon an eminence, and look down upon the world as if already enskied and sainted ; and yet when brought in contact with that world which she inwardly despises, she shrinks back with all the timidity natural to her cloistral education.

This union of natural grace and grandeur with the habits and sentiments of a recluse—of austerity of life with gentleness of manner—of inflexible moral principle with humility and even bashfulness of deportment—is delineated with the most beautiful and wonderful consistency. Thus when her brother sends to her, to entreat her mediation, her first feeling is fear, and a distrust in her own powers :

> " Alas ! what poor ability 's in me
> To do him good ?
> *Lucio.* Assay the power you have.
> *Isabella.* My power? Alas, I doubt."

In the first scene with Angelo she seems divided between her love for her brother and her sense of his fault ; between her self-respect and her maidenly bashfulness. She begins with a kind of hesitation " at war 'twixt will and will not :" and when Angelo quotes the law, and insists on the justice of his sentence, and the responsibility of his station, her native sense of moral rectitude and severe principles takes the lead, and she shrinks back :

> " O just but severe law !
> I *had* a brother, then.   Heaven keep your honour !"   (*Retiring.*)

Excited and encouraged by Lucio, and supported by her own natural spirit, she returns to the charge. She gains energy and self - possession as she proceeds, grows more earnest and passionate from the difficulty she encounters, and displays that eloquence and power of reasoning for which we had been already prepared by Claudio's first allusion to her :

> " In her youth
> There is a prone and speechless dialect,
> Such as moves men ; beside, she hath prosperous art,
> When she will play with reason and discourse,
> And well she can persuade."

It is a curious coincidence that Isabella, exhorting Angelo to mercy, avails herself of precisely the same arguments and insists on the self-same topics which Portia addresses to Shylock in her celebrated speech ; but how beautifully and how truly is the distinction marked! how like, and yet how unlike! Portia's eulogy on mercy is a piece of heavenly rhetoric ; it falls on the ear with a solemn measured harmony ; it is the voice of a descended angel addressing an inferior nature : if not premeditated, it is at least part of a preconcerted scheme ; while Isabella's pleadings are poured from the abundance of her heart in broken sentences, and with the artless vehemence of one who feels that life and death hang upon her appeal. This will be best understood by placing the corresponding passages in immediate comparison with each other.

> "*Portia.* The quality of mercy is not strain'd,
> It droppeth as the gentle rain from heaven
> Upon the place beneath ; it is twice blest ;
> It blesseth him that gives and him that takes ;
> 'T is mightiest in the mightiest ; it becomes
> The throned monarch better than his crown :
> His sceptre shows the force of temporal power,
> The attribute to awe and majesty,
> Wherein doth sit the dread and fear of kings ;
> But mercy is above this sceptred sway ;
> It is enthroned in the hearts of kings."

> "*Isabella.*   Well, believe this,
> No ceremony that to great ones longs,
> Not the king's crown, nor the deputed sword,
> The marshal's truncheon, nor the judge's robe,
> Become them with one half so good a grace
> As mercy does."

> "*Portia.*   Consider this,—
> That, in the course of justice, none of us
> Should see salvation : we do pray for mercy;
> And that same prayer doth teach us all to render
> The deeds of mercy."
>
>   "*Isabella.*   Alas, alas !
> Why all the souls that were were forfeit once ;
> And He that might the vantage best have took
> Found out the remedy.   How would you be,
> If He, which is the top of judgment, should
> But judge you as you are ?   O, think on that !
> And mercy then will breathe within your lips,
> Like man new made."

The beautiful things which Isabella is made to utter have, like the sayings of Portia, become proverbial ; but in spirit and character they are as distinct as are the two women. In all that Portia says, we confess the power of a rich, poetical imagination, blended with a quick practical spirit of observation, familiar with the surfaces of things ; while there is a profound yet simple morality, a depth of religious feeling, a touch of melancholy, in Isabella's sentiments, and something earnest and authoritative in the manner and expression, as though they had grown up in her mind from long and deep meditation in the silence and solitude of her convent cell. . . .

Isabella's confession of the general frailty of her sex has a peculiar softness, beauty, and propriety.   She admits the imputation with all the sympathy of woman for woman ; yet with all the dignity of one who felt her own superiority to the weakness she acknowledges.

> "*Angelo.* Nay, women are frail, too.
> *Isabella.* Ay, as the glasses where they view themselves,
> Which are as easy broke as they make forms.
> Women ! Help heaven ! men their creation mar
> In profiting by them. Nay, call us ten times frail ;
> For we are soft as our complexions are,
> And credulous to false prints."

Nor should we fail to remark the deeper interest which is thrown round Isabella by one part of her character, which is betrayed rather than exhibited in the progress of the action; and for which we are not at first prepared, though it is so perfectly natural. It is the strong undercurrent of passion and enthusiasm flowing beneath this calm and saintly self-possession; it is the capacity for high feeling and generous and strong indignation, veiled beneath the sweet austere composure of the religious recluse, which, by the very force of contrast, powerfully impress the imagination. As we see in real life that where, from some external or habitual cause, a strong control is exercised over naturally quick feelings and an impetuous temper, they display themselves with a proportionate vehemence when that restraint is removed; so the very violence with which her passions burst forth, when opposed or under the influence of strong excitement, is admirably characteristic.

Thus in her exclamation, when she first allows herself to perceive Angelo's vile design—

> " Ha ! little honour to be much believ'd,
> And most pernicious purpose ! Seeming, seeming !
> I will proclaim thee, Angelo ; look for it !
> Sign me a present pardon for my brother,
> Or with an outstretch'd throat I 'll tell the world
> Aloud what man thou art."

And again, where she finds that the "outward sainted deputy" has deceived her—

> " O, I will to him, and pluck out his eyes !
> Unhappy Claudio ! wretched Isabel !
> Injurious world ! most damned Angelo !"

She places at first a strong and high-souled confidence in her brother's fortitude and magnanimity, judging him by her own lofty spirit; but when her trust in his honour is deceived by his momentary weakness, her scorn has a bitterness and her indignation a force of expression almost fearful; and

both are carried to an extreme which is perfectly in character. . . .

The whole of this scene with Claudio is inexpressibly
grand in the poetry and the sentiment; and the entire play
abounds in those passages and phrases which must have become trite from familiar and constant use and abuse, if their
wisdom and unequalled beauty did not invest them with an
immortal freshness and vigour and a perpetual charm. . . .

Of all the characters, Isabella alone has our sympathy.
But though she triumphs in the conclusion, her triumph is
not produced in a pleasing manner. There are too many
disguises and tricks, too many "by-paths and indirect
crooked ways," to conduct us to the natural and foreseen
catastrophe, which the duke's presence throughout renders
inevitable. This duke seems to have a predilection for
bringing about justice by a most unjustifiable succession of
falsehoods and counterplots. He really deserves Lucio's
satirical designation, who somewhere styles him "the fantastical duke of dark corners." But Isabella is ever con-
sistent in her pure and upright simplicity, and, in the midst
of this simulation, expresses a characteristic disapprobation
of the part she is made to play:

> "To speak so indirectly I am loath;
> I would say the truth."

She yields to the supposed friar with a kind of forced
docility, because her situation as a religious novice, and his
station, habit, and authority, as her spiritual director, demand
this sacrifice. In the end we are made to feel that her tran-
sition from the convent to the throne has but placed this
noble creature in her natural sphere; for though Isabella as
Duchess of Vienna could not more command our highest
reverence than Isabella the novice of St. Clare, yet a wider
range of usefulness and benevolence, of trial and action, was
better suited to the large capacity, the ardent affections, the

energetic intellect, and firm **principle** of such a woman **as** Isabella than the **walls of a cloister.** The ·philosophical duke observes in the very first scene :

> "Spirits are not finely touch'd
> But to fine issues, nor Nature never lends
> The smallest scruple of her excellence
> But, like a thrifty goddess, she determines
> Herself the glory of a creditor,
> Both thanks and use."

This profound and beautiful sentiment is illustrated in the character and destiny of Isabella. She says, of herself, that "she has spirit to act whatever her heart approves;" and what her heart approves we know.

*[From Verplanck's "Shakespeare." *]*

This [the date of "the close of 1603 or the beginning of 1604"] places this remarkable drama at the commencement of that portion of the author's life, from 1602 to 1607, which was memorable for the production of *Othello*, with its bitter passion; the additions to the original *Hamlet*, with their melancholy wisdom ; probably of *Timon*, with his indignant and hearty scorn, and rebukes of the baseness of civilized society ; and, above all, of *Lear*, with its dark pictures of un-mixed, unmitigated guilt, and its terrible and prophet - like denunciations. Like all these, and perhaps more than any of them, it bears the stamp of that period of the author's life, first noted by Hallam, when some sad **influence** weighed upon the poet's spirit, and prompted him constantly to ap-pear as "the stern censurer of man." I see no reason to doubt that this did not **arise merely from a** change of taste, or an experiment in **dramatic art, but was, in some** manner, connected with **events or circumstances personal to the** author, and affecting his temper, disposition, and moral asso-

---

* *The Illustrated Shakespeare*, edited by G. C. Verplanck (New York, 1847), vol. ii. p. 4 of *M. for M.*

ciations of thought. There is no part of the author's own practical philosophy more true than that "a man's mind is parcel of his fortunes." He does not, indeed, like Milton, or Rousseau, or Byron, delight to make himself the prominent figure in all his intellectual creations; yet these are not the less evidently coloured by the varying moods predominant, from time to time, during the changes of life. Few men could have more enjoyed life, or have more intensely relished the beautiful or the pleasurable, or more revelled in the ludicrous and the fantastical, than the author of that gay and bright succession of poetic comedies, from *Love's Labour 's Lost* to *As You Like It* and the *Twelfth Night.* How striking is the contrast, in this respect, between these, and especially between the last—and to my taste the most delightful of all—and the *Measure for Measure*, austere in its ethical poetry, and sarcastic in its humorous delineations! or between this last and *The Merchant of Venice*, where the same topics are often enforced, the same train of thought and even of imagery introduced! They are the same, yet how different!—like the same landscape seen in the sparkling sunshine, after a vernal rain, and again under a lowering wintry sky. The cause must remain in darkness; but, to my mind, it appears manifest that the effect was not the result merely of altering taste or ripening judgment. *Samson Agonistes* does not more strongly testify to some great and overwhelming physical and political revolution prostrating and fettering the intellectual giant, in body and mind, than this play and the nearly contemporary writings of its author do to some similar moral cause, or some external calamity of life acting upon the moral faculties, and producing new combinations and results in Shakespeare's moral anatomy of the human heart. It may have been some deep wound of the affections, some repeated evidence of man's ingratitude and heartlessness, possibly some mere personal calamity, bringing home to the brilliant and successful man of genius the living sense of the world's worthlessness, and opening to his sight the mysterious evil of his own nature.

Whatever, then, may have been the immediate and external causes of this signal intellectual phenomenon in our literary history, it is undeniable that this drama of *Measure for Measure* specially marks the period of this great climacteric of Shakespeare's genius, resembling those climacterics of the body which, according to the old notions of philosophy or superstition, come in their regular periods over man, working a strange alteration in the functions of his body, as different planets succeed with new influences to rule his mind and his destiny. Although under its strong influence the poet was now about to enter upon a nobler course of labour, and to teach the world deeper and truer lessons in the learning of "human dealings," yet we cannot but rejoice that this solemn change of all the poet's lighter fancies into something still more "rich and strange" came not until after the quick and brilliant succession of his matchless poetic comedies had perpetuated the memory of his years of buoyant spirits, hope, joy, and untiring fancy. For although we often find in his later works a calm and serene spirit of enjoyment, such as we have before alluded to in the pastoral beauties of Perdita's conversation, and the mountain scenes of *Cymbeline*—though his comic sketches in his later dramas prove that his perception of whimsical or absurd character was as acute and active as ever, and his power of graphic delineation as vivid—yet even then there seems to be an absence of that personal abandonment of the author's own spirit to the beauty or the humour of the scene to which he had before accustomed us. He appears more as the great philosophical artist, depicting the very truth and nature of his scenes, and not, as was his former wont, as himself one of his own joyous throng, mixing in the plot against the bachelor liberty of Benedick—enjoying the frolics in Eastcheap as much as Falstaff or the Prince—or joining his own voice in the boisterous glee of Sir Toby and Sir Andrew.

But *Measure for Measure* breathes a sterner spirit than belongs to the productions of either the earlier or the later periods. Dr. Johnson has said that its "comic scenes are natural and pleasing." Their fidelity to nature cannot, indeed, be denied. But if they please, they do so from their faithfulness of portraiture ; not, like the scenes of Bottom or Falstaff, and their companions, from their exuberance of mirthful sport, or their rich originality of invention and wit. They, as well as the loftier scenes of the piece, are but too faithful pictures of the degrading and hardening influence of licentious passion, from the lighter profligacy of Lucio, the dissipated gentleman, to the grosser and contented degradation of the Clown ; and if these are all painted with the truth of Hogarth or Crabbe, they are depicted with no air of sport or mirth, but rather with that of bitter scorn. The author seems to smile like his own Cassius, "as if he mocked himself." Thus Elbow, in his self-satisfied conceit and pedantic ignorance, would appear, as some of the critics regard him, simply as an inferior version of Dogberry. But he is not a Dogberry in whose absurdities the author himself luxuriates, but one whose peculiarities are delineated with a contemptuous sneer. Lucio, again, is a character unfortunately too common in civilized, and especially in city, life—a gentleman in manners and education, and of good natural ability, made frivolous in mind and debased in sentiment and disposition by licentious and idle habits—thus substantially not a very different character from some of the lighter personages of the prior dramas; but he differs mainly from them because exhibited under a very different light, and regarded in a different temper. The others are represented in his scenes as they appeared to the transient acquaintance, or the companions of their pleasures. But the poet looks deeper into the heart and life of Lucio, and portrays this man of pleasure in the same mood which governs the higher and more tragic scenes of this drama — a mood sometimes contemptuous, sometimes sad, often indignant, but never such as had been his former wont, either merely playful or imaginative. Thus it seems to me that, if his comic scenes excite mirth from their truth, it is a mirth in which the author did not participate; and their sarcastic humour assimilates itself in feeling to that of the stern and grave interest of the plot, and the strong passion of its poetic scenes. Characters, in themselves light and amusing, are branded with contempt from the degradation of licentious habits; while the same passion, in a form of less grossness, but of deeper guilt, prostrates before it high reputation, talent, and wisdom. The intellectual and amiable Claudio, willing to purchase "the weariest and most loathed worldly life," at any cost of shame and sin, is strangely contrasted with the drunken Barnardine, " careless, reckless, and fearless of what is past, present, or to come." Indeed, the higher characters are mainly discriminated from the lower ones, in this moral delineation, in that conscience is dull or dead in the latter, while it appears in all its terrors in Angelo and Claudio, and in all the majesty of purity in Isabella. There is little formality of moral instruction, but the secret workings of guilt and fear are laid open with the rapidity, suddenness, and brevity of unuttered and half-formed thoughts. That men of lax moral opinions should shrink with disgust, as some of his critics have done, from this too true a delineation of so common a vice, is not to be wondered at. It was less to be expected that Coleridge should have formed the judgment he has expressed on this drama, though there are not a few readers who will assent to it. He observes, in his *Literary Remains:* "This play, which is Shakespeare's throughout, is to me the most painful, say rather the only painful, part of his genuine works. The comic and tragic parts equally border on the *miseteon*— the one being disgusting, the other horrible; and the pardon and marriage of Angelo not merely baffles the strong, indignant claim of justice (for cruelty, with lust and damnable baseness, cannot be forgiven, because we cannot conceive them as being morally repented of), but it is likewise degrading to the character of woman." We also learn from Mr. Collier that, in the course of lectures on Shakespeare delivered in 1818 (which were delivered from imperfect notes, and never written out), Coleridge pointed especially to the artifice of Isabella, and her seeming consent to the suit of Angelo, as the circumstances which tended to lower the character of the female sex. He then called *Measure for Measure* only the " least agreeable " of Shakespeare's dramas.

This criticism, however little laudatory, is still substantially an acknowledgment of the severe unity of feeling and purpose which pervades the piece, and the impressive power with which it enforces revolting and humbling truths. These are the more conspicuous, because the dark painting of moral degradation, of guilt, remorse, and the dread of death, is not relieved, as is the poet's use elsewhere, by passages of descriptive beauty, or fancy, or tenderness. The only strong contrast which supplies their place is that of the severe beauty of Isabella's character, and the majestic wisdom and deep sentiment of her fervid eloquence. That in this sense the drama is not agreeable, and that it is even painful, is very true; yet the degree of pain thus given is precisely that by which the intellect is most excited, and which is thus the source of the deep and absorbing interest excited by all gloomy yet true pictures of life, in its sadder shapes of crime and woe. Though the subject and the thoughts be in themselves repulsive, yet when, as here, we feel that the author is breathing through them the strong emotions of his own soul, the attention is fixed, and the sympathy enchained. This is the secret of Dante's power, and of that of the nobler portion of Byron's poetry. That *Measure for Measure* possesses much of this power, is proved by the fact that, in spite of the objections of critics of every degree, it has always taken a strong hold of the general mind. No one of the high female

characters of tragedy has been found more effective in representation than Isabella; while there is perhaps no composition of the same length in the language which has left
more of its expressive phrases, its moral aphorisms, its brief
sentences crowded with meaning, fixed in the general memory, and embodied by daily use in every form of popular
eloquence, argument, and literature.

[*From Mr. F. J. Furnivall's Introduction to the Play.**]

On the stifling air of this drama, as contrasted with earlier
ones, hear Mr. W. Watkiss Lloyd : " We never throughout
this play get into the free, open, joyous atmosphere so invig-
orating in other works of Shakspere : the oppressive gloom
of the prison, the foul breath of the brothel, are only ex-
changed for the chilly damp of conventual walls, or the oppressive retirement of the monastery, where friars are curious
as to the motives of ducal seclusion, and are ready to intimate that a petticoat is concerned in the secret." Yet
though we have this " night's black curtain " over the play ;†
though woman's and man's incontinence match, to some extent, the queen's and Claudius's in *Hamlet;* though Claudio
in his weak fear of death, like Hamlet, fails to do his duty ;
yet here, beside, in intentional contrast to the lust and weak
will of woman and man, rises, like the moon in its pure
beauty, like the lightning-flash in its white wrath, the noble
figure of Isabella, " a thing enskied and sainted, an immortal
spirit," Shakspere's first wholly Christian woman, steadfast
and true as Portia, Brutus's wife, pure as Lucrece's soul,
merciful above Portia, Bassanio's bride, in that she prays for
forgiveness for her foe, not her friend; with an unyielding
will, a martyr's spirit above Helena's of *All 's Well,* the highest type of woman that Shakspere has yet drawn. . . .

* *The Leopold Shakspere* (London, 1877), p. lxxiv.
† The play was probably written during the plague of 1603 in London,
in which, according to Stowe, 30,578 persons died.

Those who would put *Measure for Measure* next to *All 's Well** surely overlook the far deeper tone of the former play: its dealing with death and the future world, its weight of reflection, the analysis of Angelo's character, the working of conscience, the greater corruption dealt with, the higher saintliness shown in Isabella. Also, if we look at the name of the play, *Measure for Measure*, we shall see that Shakspere's idea in it was, though with grim humour and ultimate relenting, to preach in Angelo and Lucio his Third-Period doctrine—an eye for an eye, a tooth for a tooth, vengeance for weakness, yielding to temptation and sin, though here the vengeance is but the poetical justice of marriage to the women whom the sinners have sinned with or abandoned. Intending nun as Isabella is, we must nevertheless look on her as no hard recluse, but as " Isabel, sweet Isabel," with cheek-roses, gentle and fair. Yet she is "a thing enskied and sainted, an immortal spirit ;" and this enables us to understand the conflict that must have gone on in her mind between her sisterly affection and her religious principles when pleading her brother's cause, and her acquiescence in Angelo's resolve that Claudio must die. Both times she needs Lucio's appeal before she 'll again urge how much better mercy becomes the king and judge than justice. Her unhappy words, " Hark ! how I 'll bribe you," seem to have first brought out the evil in Angelo. " He tempts her through that which is uppermost in the noble woman, the passion for sacrifice. There is something splendid in the idea of perilling the soul itself for the sake of another " (E. H. Hickey). Shakspere's original, Whetstone, makes his heroine Cassandra give way to her brother's appeal :

> " My Andrugio, take comfort in distresse ;
> Cassandra is wonne, thy rannsome greate to paye."

---

* Mr. Furnivall puts *M. for M.* next to *Hamlet* in the order of the plays. See p. 11 above.—*Ed.*

But this was not Shakspere's conception of Isabella. She believed that the son of her heroic father was noble like herself; and when she found that he was willing to sacrifice her honour for his life, " her swift vindictive anger leapt like a white flame from her white spirit," * and her indignant "take my defiance, die, perish," was her fit answer to her brother's base proposal. Yet she who would not stoop to wrong, dared for the sake of Mariana to bear the imputation of it. She had no care for the world's opinion, so that the deed appeared not foul in the truth of her spirit ; and as in *The Merry Wives* and *Much Ado*, her quick woman's wit took a righteous delight in circumventing a knave. We have another passionate outburst from her when she hears the false news that her brother has been executed. And then she takes her side by the duke, who loves her, to fight with him God's fight against the evil in that foul Vienna ; a far better post, heading Heaven's army in her land, than praying barren prayers in convent walls. She is the first of the three splendid women who illumine the dark Third Period : she, glorious for her purity and righteousness, Cordelia for her truth and filial love, Volumnia for her devotion to honour and her love of her native land. Perhaps we may add a fourth, Portia, Brutus's wife, for nobleness and wifely duty. But the highest of all is Isabella.

* See my friend Mr. W. H. Pater's admirable paper in *The Fortnightly Review*, 1874 or 1875.

C

ROOM IN WHICH TRADITION SAYS SHAKESPEARE WAS BORN.

MEASURE FOR MEASURE.

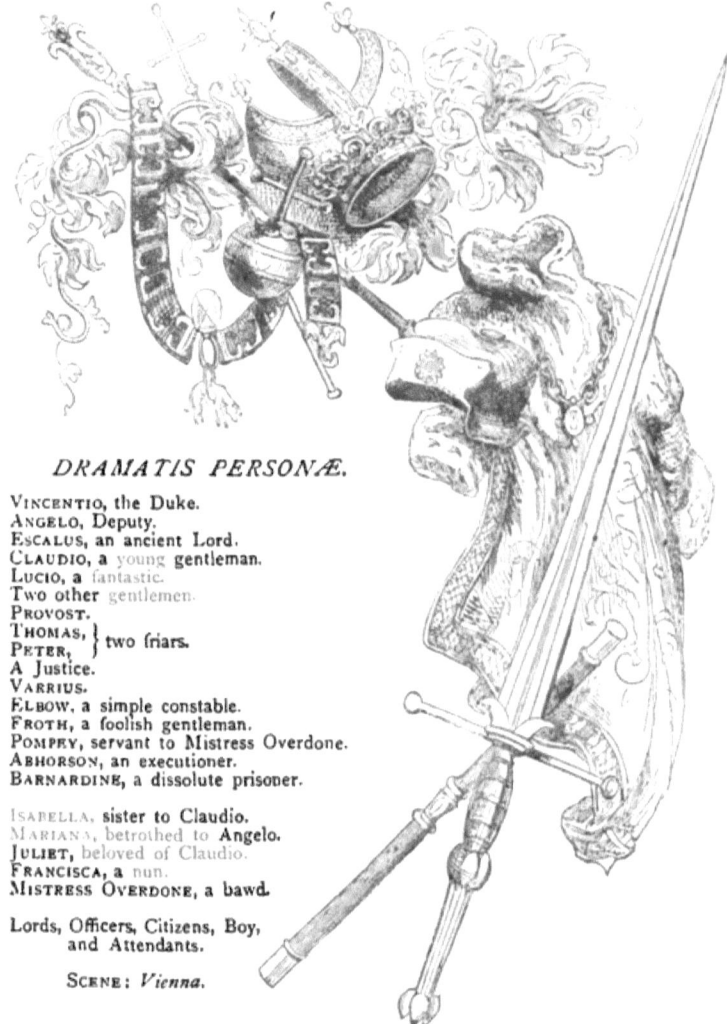

DRAMATIS PERSONÆ.

VINCENTIO, the Duke.
ANGELO, Deputy.
ESCALUS, an ancient Lord.
CLAUDIO, a young gentleman.
LUCIO, a fantastic.
Two other gentlemen.
PROVOST.
THOMAS, } two friars.
PETER,
A Justice.
VARRIUS.
ELBOW, a simple constable.
FROTH, a foolish gentleman.
POMPEY, servant to Mistress Overdone.
ABHORSON, an executioner.
BARNARDINE, a dissolute prisoner.

ISABELLA, sister to Claudio.
MARIANA, betrothed to Angelo.
JULIET, beloved of Claudio.
FRANCISCA, a nun.
MISTRESS OVERDONE, a bawd.

Lords, Officers, Citizens, Boy,
    and Attendants.

SCENE: *Vienna.*

STREET IN VIENNA (SCENE III.).

ACT I.

SCENE I. *An Apartment in the Duke's Palace.*

Enter DUKE, ESCALUS, Lords *and* Attendants.

Duke. Escalus.

Escalus. My lord.

Duke. Of government the properties to unfold
Would seem in me to affect speech and discourse,
Since I am put to know that your own science
Exceeds, in that, the lists of all advice
My strength can give you ; then no more remains

But that to your sufficiency—as your worth is able—
And let them work.   The nature of our people,
Our city's institutions, and the terms   10
For common justice, you 're as pregnant in
As art and practice hath enriched any
That we remember.   There is our commission,
From which we would not have you warp.—Call hither,
I say, bid come before us Angelo.—   [*Exit an Attendant.*
What figure of us think you he will bear?
For you must know, we have with special soul
Elected him our absence to supply,
Lent him our terror, dress'd him with our love,
And given his deputation all the organs   20
Of our own power.   What think you of it?
    Escalus. If any in Vienna be of worth
To undergo such ample grace and honour,
It is Lord Angelo.
    Duke.   Look where he comes.

Enter ANGELO.

    Angelo. Always obedient to your grace's will,
I come to know your pleasure.
    Duke.   Angelo,
There is a kind of character in thy life,
That to the observer doth thy history
Fully unfold.   Thyself and thy belongings
Are not thine own so proper as to waste   30
Thyself upon thy virtues, they on thee.
Heaven doth with us as we with torches do,
Not light them for themselves; for if our virtues
Did not go forth of us, 't were all alike
As if we had them not.   Spirits are not finely touch'd
But to fine issues, nor Nature never lends
The smallest scruple of her excellence
But, like a thrifty goddess, she determines

Herself the glory of a creditor,
Both thanks and use.   But I do bend my speech   40
To one that can my part in him advertise ;
Hold therefore, Angelo :—
In our remove be thou at full ourself;
Mortality and mercy in Vienna
Live in thy tongue and heart.   Old Escalus,
Though first in question, is thy secondary.
Take thy commission.
   Angelo.   Now, good my lord,
Let there be some more test made of my metal,
Before so noble and so great a figure
Be stamp'd upon it.
   Duke.   No more evasion :   50
We have with a leaven'd and prepared choice
Proceeded to you ; therefore take your honours.
Our haste from hence is of so quick condition
That it prefers itself and leaves unquestion'd
Matters of needful value.   We shall write to you,
As time and our concernings shall importune,
How it goes with us, and do look to know
What doth befall you here.   So, fare you well ;
To the hopeful execution do I leave you
Of your commissions.
   Angelo.   Yet give leave, my lord,   60
That we may bring you something on the way.
   Duke. My haste may not admit it :
Nor need you, on mine honour, have to do
With any scruple ; your scope is as mine own,
So to enforce or qualify the laws
As to your soul seems good.   Give me your hand.
I 'll privily away.   I love the people,
But do not like to stage me to their eyes.
Though it do well, I do not relish well
Their loud applause and aves vehement ;   70

Nor do I think the man of safe discretion
That does affect it.   Once more, fare you well.
Angelo. The heavens give safety to your purposes !
Escalus. Lead forth and bring you back in happiness !
Duke. I thank you.   Fare you well.   [*Exit.*
Escalus. I shall desire you, sir, to give me leave
To have free speech with you; and it concerns me
To look into the bottom of my place.
A power I have, but of what strength and nature
I am not yet instructed.   80
Angelo. 'T is so with me.   Let us withdraw together,
And we may soon our satisfaction have
Touching that point.
Escalus. I 'll wait upon your honour.   [*Exeunt.*

SCENE II.   *A Street.*

Enter LUCIO *and two* Gentlemen.

Lucio. If the duke with the other dukes come not to composition with the King of Hungary, why then all the dukes
fall upon the king.

1 *Gentleman.* Heaven grant us its peace, but not the King
of Hungary's !

2 *Gentleman.* Amen.

Lucio. Thou concludest like the sanctimonious pirate, that
went to sea with the Ten Commandments, but scraped one
out of the table.

2 *Gentleman.* Thou shalt not steal?   10

Lucio. Ay, that he razed.

1 *Gentleman.* Why, 't was a commandment to command
the captain and all the rest from their functions ; they put
forth to steal.   There 's not a soldier of us all, that, in the
thanksgiving before meat, do relish the petition well that
prays for peace.

2 *Gentleman.* I never heard any soldier dislike it.

Lucio. I believe thee ; for I think thou never wast where grace was said.

2 *Gentleman.* No? a dozen times at least. 20

1 *Gentleman.* What, in metre?

Lucio. In any proportion or in any language.

1 *Gentleman.* I think, or in any religion.

Lucio. Ay, why not? Grace is grace, despite of all controversy; as, for example, thou thyself art a wicked villain, despite of all grace.

1 *Gentleman.* Well, there went but a pair of shears between us.

Lucio. I grant; as there may between the lists and the velvet. Thou art the list. 30

1 *Gentleman.* And thou the velvet: thou art good velvet; thou 'rt a three-piled piece, I warrant thee. I had as lief be a list of an English kersey as be piled, as thou art piled, for a French velvet. Do I speak feelingly now?

Lucio. I think thou dost; and, indeed, with most painful feeling of thy speech. I will, out of thine own confession, learn to begin thy health ; but, whilst I live, forget to drink after thee.

1 *Gentleman.* I think I have done myself wrong, have I not? 40

2 *Gentleman.* Yes, that thou hast, whether thou art tainted or free.

Lucio. Behold, behold, where Madam Mitigation comes !

1 *Gentleman.* I have purchased as many diseases under her roof as come to—

2 *Gentleman.* To what, I pray?

Lucio. Judge.

2 *Gentleman.* To three thousand dolours a year.

1 *Gentleman.* Ay, and more.

Lucio. A French crown more. 50

1 *Gentleman.* Thou art always figuring diseases in me ; but thou art full of error ; I am sound.

Lucio. Nay, not as one would say, healthy; but so sound as things that are hollow : thy bones are hollow; impiety has made a feast of thee.

Enter MISTRESS OVERDONE.

1 *Gentleman.* How now! which of your hips has the most profound sciatica?

Mrs. Overdone. Well, well; there 's one yonder arrested and carried to prison was worth five thousand of you all.

2 *Gentleman.* Who 's that, I pray thee?   60

Mrs. Overdone. Marry, sir, that 's Claudio, Signior Claudio.

1 *Gentleman.* Claudio to prison! 't is not so.

Mrs. Overdone. Nay, but I know 't is so. I saw him arrested, saw him carried away; and, which is more, within these three days his head to be chopped off.

Lucio. But, after all this fooling, I would not have it so. Art thou sure of this?

Mrs. Overdone. I am too sure of it; and it is for getting Madam Julietta with child.   69

Lucio. Believe me, this may be ; he promised to meet me two hours since, and he was ever precise in promise-keeping.

2 *Gentleman.* Besides, you know, it draws something near to the speech we had to such a purpose.

1 *Gentleman.* But, most of all, agreeing with the proclamation.

Lucio. Away! let 's go learn the truth of it.

[*Exeunt Lucio and Gentlemen.*

Mrs. Overdone. Thus, what with the war, what with the sweat, what with the gallows, and what with poverty, I am custom-shrunk.—

Enter POMPEY.

How now! what 's the news with you?   80

Pompey. Yonder man is carried to prison.

Mrs. Overdone. Well, what has he done?

Pompey. A woman.

Mrs. Overdone. What, is there a maid with child by him?

Pompey. No, but there 's a woman with maid by him. You have not heard of the proclamation, have you?

Mrs. Overdone. What proclamation, man?

Pompey. All houses in the suburbs of Vienna must be plucked down.

Mrs. Overdone. And what shall become of those in the city?   91

Pompey. They shall stand for seed; they had gone down too, but that a wise burgher put in for them.

Mrs. Overdone. But shall all our houses of resort in the suburbs be pulled down?

Pompey. To the ground, mistress.

Mrs. Overdone. Why, here 's a change indeed in the commonwealth? What shall become of me?

Pompey. Come, fear not you; good counsellors lack no clients. Though you change your place, you need not change your trade; I 'll be your tapster still. Courage! there will be pity taken on you; you that have worn your eyes almost out in the service, you will be considered.   103

Mrs. Overdone. What 's to do here, Thomas Tapster? let 's withdraw.

Pompey. Here comes Signior Claudio, led by the provost to prison; and there 's Madam Juliet.   [*Exeunt.*

Enter PROVOST, CLAUDIO, JULIET, *and* Officers.

Claudio. Fellow, why dost thou show me thus to the world? Bear me to prison, where I am committed.

Provost. I do it not in evil disposition,   110
But from Lord Angelo by special charge.

Claudio. Thus can the demigod Authority
Make us pay down for our offence by weight.—
The words of heaven:—on whom it will, it will;
On whom it will not, so; yet still 't is just.

Re-enter Lucio *and two* Gentlemen.

Lucio. Why, how now, Claudio! whence comes this restraint?

Claudio. From too much liberty, my Lucio, liberty;
As surfeit is the father of much fast,
So every scope by the immoderate use
Turns to restraint.   Our natures do pursue,   120
Like rats that ravin down their proper bane,
A thirsty evil; and when we drink we die.

Lucio. If I could speak so wisely under an arrest, I would
send for certain of my creditors; and yet, to say the truth, I
had as lief have the foppery of freedom as the morality of
imprisonment.   What 's thy offence, Claudio?

Claudio. What but to speak of would offend again.

Lucio. What, is 't murther?

Claudio. No.

Lucio. Lechery?   130

Claudio. Call it so.

Provost. Away, sir! you must go.

Claudio. One word, good friend.—Lucio, a word with you.

Lucio. A hundred, if they 'll do you any good.—Is lechery
     so look'd after?

Claudio. Thus stands it with me: upon a true contract
I got possession of Julietta's bed.
You know the lady; she is fast my wife,
Save that we do the denunciation lack
Of outward order: this we came not to,
Only for propagation of a dower   140
Remaining in the coffer of her friends,
From whom we thought it meet to hide our love
Till time had made them for us.   But it chances
The stealth of our most mutual entertainment
With character too gross is writ on Juliet.

Lucio. With child, perhaps?

Claudio.   Unhappily, even so.
And the new deputy now for the duke—
Whether it be the fault and glimpse of newness,
Or whether that the body public be
A horse whereon the governor doth ride,   150
Who, newly in the seat, that it may know
He can command, lets it straight feel the spur;
Whether the tyranny be in his place,
Or in his eminence that fills it up,
I stagger in:—but this new governor
Awakes me all the enrolled penalties
Which have, like unscour'd armour, hung by the wall
So long that nineteen zodiacs have gone round
And none of them been worn ; and, for a name,
Now puts the drowsy and neglected act   160
Freshly on me: 't is surely for a name.

Lucio. I warrant it is; and thy head stands so tickle on
thy shoulders that a milkmaid, if she be in love, may sigh it
off.   Send after the duke and appeal to him.

Claudio. I have done so, but he 's not to be found.
I prithee, Lucio, do me this kind service.
This day my sister should the cloister enter
And there receive her approbation:
Acquaint her with the danger of my state ;
Implore her, in my voice, that she make friends   170
To the strict deputy ; bid herself assay him.
I have great hope in that ; for in her youth
There is a prone and speechless dialect,
Such as move men ; beside, she hath prosperous art
When she will play with reason and discourse,
And well she can persuade.

Lucio. I pray she may ; as well for the encouragement of
the like, which else would stand under grievous imposition,
as for the enjoying of thy life, who I would be sorry should
be thus foolishly lost at a game of tick-tack.   I 'll to her.

Claudio. I thank you, good friend Lucio.   181
Lucio. Within two hours.
Claudio.   Come, officer, away ! [*Exeunt.*

SCENE III. *A Monastery.*

Enter DUKE *and* FRIAR THOMAS.

Duke. No, holy father; throw away that thought;
Believe not that the dribbling dart of love
Can pierce a complete bosom. Why I desire thee
To give me secret harbour, hath a purpose
More grave and wrinkled than the aims and ends
Of burning youth.
 Friar Thomas.   May your grace speak of it?
 Duke. My holy sir, none better knows than you
How I have ever lov'd the life remov'd,
And held in idle price to haunt assemblies
Where youth, and cost, and witless bravery keeps.   10
I have deliver'd to Lord Angelo,
A man of stricture and firm abstinence,
My absolute power and place here in Vienna,
And he supposes me travell'd to Poland ;
For so I have strew'd it in the common ear,
And so it is receiv'd. Now, pious sir,
You will demand of me why I do this?
 Friar Thomas. Gladly, my lord.
 Duke. We have strict statutes and most biting laws,
The needful bits and curbs to headstrong steeds,   20
Which for this fourteen years we have let sleep,
Even like an o'ergrown lion in a cave,
That goes not out to prey. Now, as fond fathers,
Having bound up the threatening twigs of birch,
Only to stick it in their children's sight
For terror, not to use, in time the rod
Becomes more mock'd than fear'd ; so our decrees,

Dead to infliction, to themselves are dead,
And liberty plucks justice by the nose;
The baby beats the nurse, and quite athwart   30
Goes all decorum.
  Friar Thomas.   It rested in your grace
To unloose this tied-up justice when you pleas'd:
And it in you more dreadful would have seem'd
Than in Lord Angelo.
  Duke.   I do fear, too dreadful.
Sith 't was my fault to give the people scope,
'T would be my tyranny to strike and gall them
For what I bid them do; for we bid this be done,
When evil deeds have their permissive pass
And not the punishment. Therefore, indeed, my father,
I have on Angelo impos'd the office;   40
Who may, in the ambush of my name, strike home,
And yet my nature never in the fight
To do me slander. And to behold his sway,
I will, as 't were a brother of your order,
Visit both prince and people; therefore, I prithee,
Supply me with the habit, and instruct me
How I may formally in person bear me
Like a true friar. More reasons for this action
At our more leisure shall I render you;
Only, this one: Lord Angelo is precise,   50
Stands at a guard with envy, scarce confesses
That his blood flows or that his appetite
Is more to bread than stone; hence shall we see,
If power change purpose, what our seemers be.   [*Exeunt.*

SCENE IV.   *A Nunnery.*

Enter ISABELLA *and* FRANCISCA.

Isabella. And have you nuns no farther privileges?
Francisca. Are not these large enough?

Isabella. Yes, truly; I speak not as desiring more,
But rather wishing a more strict restraint
Upon the sisterhood, the votarists of Saint Clare.
  Lucio. [*Within*] Ho!   Peace be in this place!
  Isabella.   Who 's that which calls?
Francisca. It is a man's voice.   Gentle Isabella,
Turn you the key, and know his business of him.
You may, I may not; you are yet unsworn.
When you have vow'd, you must not speak with men   10
But in the presence of the prioress;
Then, if you speak, you must not show your face,
Or, if you show your face, you must not speak.
He calls again; I pray you, answer him.   [*Exit.*
  Isabella. Peace and prosperity!   Who is 't that calls?

Enter LUCIO.

  Lucio. Hail, virgin, if you be, as those cheek-roses
Proclaim you are no less!   Can you so stead me
As bring me to the sight of Isabella,
A novice of this place and the fair sister
To her unhappy brother Claudio?   20
  Isabella. Why her unhappy brother? let me ask,
The rather for I now must make you know
I am that Isabella and his sister.
  Lucio. Gentle and fair, your brother kindly greets you.
Not to be weary with you, he 's in prison.
  Isabella. Woe me! for what?
  Lucio. For that which, if myself might be his judge,
He should receive his punishment in thanks.
He hath got his friend with child.
  Isabella. Sir, make me not your story.
  Lucio.   It is true.   30
I would not—though 't is my familiar sin
With maids to seem the lapwing and to jest,
Tongue far from heart—play with all virgins so.

I hold you as a thing enskied and sainted,
By your renouncement an immortal spirit,
And to be talk'd with in sincerity,
As with a saint.
    Isabella. You do blaspheme the good in mocking me.
    Lucio. Do not believe it.   Fewness and truth, 't is thus:
Your brother and his lover have embrac'd;   40
As those that feed grow full, as blossoming time
That from the seedness the bare fallow brings
To teeming foison, even so her plenteous womb
Expresseth his full tilth and husbandry.
    Isabella. Some one with child by him?   My cousin Juliet?
    Lucio. Is she your cousin?
    Isabella. Adoptedly; as school-maids change their names
By vain though apt affection.
    Lucio.   She it is.
    Isabella. O, let him marry her!
    Lucio.   This is the point.
The duke is very strangely gone from hence;   50
Bore many gentlemen, myself being one,
In hand and hope of action: but we do learn
By those that know the very nerves of state,
His givings-out were of an infinite distance
From his true-meant design.   Upon his place,
And with full line of his authority,
Governs Lord Angelo; a man whose blood
Is very snow-broth, one who never feels
The wanton stings and motions of the sense,
But doth rebate and blunt his natural edge   60
With profits of the mind, study and fast.
He—to give fear to use and liberty,
Which have for long run by the hideous law,
As mice by lions—hath pick'd out an act,
Under whose heavy sense your brother's life
Falls into forfeit; he arrests him on it,
D

And follows close the rigour of the statute,
To make him an example. All hope is gone,
Unless you have the grace by your fair prayer
To soften Angelo ; and that 's my pith of business   70
'Twixt you and your poor brother.
    Isabella. Doth he so seek his life?
    Lucio.   Has censur'd him
Already ; and, as I hear, the provost hath
A warrant for his execution.
    Isabella. Alas! what poor ability 's in me
To do him good?
    Lucio.   Assay the power you have.
    Isabella. My power? Alas. I doubt—
    Lucio.   Our doubts are traitors,
And make us lose the good we oft might win
By fearing to attempt. Go to Lord Angelo,
And let him learn to know, when maidens sue,   80
Men give like gods ; but when they weep and kneel,
All their petitions are as freely theirs
As they themselves would owe them.
    Isabella. I 'll see what I can do.
    Lucio.   But speedily.
    Isabella. I will about it straight,
No longer staying but to give the mother
Notice of my affair. I humbly thank you :
Commend me to my brother ; soon at night
I 'll send him certain word of my success.
    Lucio. I take my leave of you.
    Isabella.   Good sir, adieu. [*Exeunt.*

China dishes (ii. i. 91).

ACT II.

Scene I. *A Hall in Angelo's House.*

Enter Angelo, Escalus, *and a* Justice, Provost, Officers, *and other* Attendants, *behind.*

Angelo. We must not make a scarecrow of the law,
Setting it up to fear the birds of prey,

And let it keep one shape, till custom make it
Their perch and not their terror.
 Escalus.   Ay, but yet
Let us be keen, and rather cut a little,
Than fall and bruise to death. Alas, this gentleman,
Whom I would save, had a most noble father!
Let but your honour know,
Whom I believe to be most strait in virtue,
That, in the working of your own affections,   10
Had time coher'd with place, or place with wishing,
Or that the resolute acting of your blood
Could have attain'd the effect of your own purpose,
Whether you had not sometime in your life
Err'd in this point which now you censure him,
And pull'd the law upon you.
 Angelo. 'T is one thing to be tempted, Escalus,
Another thing to fall. I not deny,
The jury, passing on the prisoner's life,
May in the sworn twelve have a thief or two   20
Guiltier than him they try. What 's open made to justice,
That justice seizes; what knows the law
That thieves do pass on thieves? 'T is very pregnant,
The jewel that we find, we stoop and take 't
Because we see it ; but what we do not see
We tread upon, and never think of it.
You may not so extenuate his offence
For I have had such faults ; but rather tell me,
When I, that censure him, do so offend,
Let mine own judgment pattern out my death,   30
And nothing come in partial. Sir, he must die.
 Escalus. Be it as your wisdom will.
 Angelo.   Where is the provost?
 Provost. Here, if it like your honour.
 Angelo.   See that Claudio
Be executed by nine to-morrow morning.

Bring him his confessor, let him be prepar'd;
For that 's the utmost of his pilgrimage.   [*Exit Provost.*
   Escalus. [*Aside*] Well, heaven forgive him! and forgive
     us all!
Some rise by sin, and some by virtue fall:
Some run from brakes of vice, and answer none;
And some condemned for a fault alone.   40

   Enter ELBOW, *and* Officers *with* FROTH *and* POMPEY.

   Elbow. Come, bring them away. If these be good
people in a commonweal that do nothing but use their
abuses in common houses, I know no law; bring them
away.

   Angelo. How now, sir! What 's your name? and what 's
the matter?

   Elbow. If it please your honour, I am the poor duke's
constable, and my name is Elbow. I do lean upon justice,
sir, and do bring in here before your good honour two notorious benefactors.   50

   Angelo. Benefactors? Well; what benefactors are they?
are they not malefactors?

   Elbow. If it please your honour, I know not well what
they are; but precise villains they are, that I am sure of,
and void of all profanation in the world that good Christians
ought to have.

   Escalus. This comes off well; here 's a wise officer.

   Angelo. Go to; what quality are they of? Elbow is your
name? why dost thou not speak, Elbow?

   Pompey. He cannot, sir; he 's out at elbow.   60

   Angelo. What are you, sir?

   Elbow. He, sir! a tapster, sir,—parcel-bawd; one that
serves a bad woman, whose house, sir, was, as they say,
plucked down in the suburbs; and now she professes a hot-
house, which, I think, is a very ill house too.

   Escalus. How know you that?

Elbow. My wife, sir, whom I detest before heaven and your honour,—

Escalus. How? thy wife?

Elbow. Ay, sir; whom, I thank heaven, is an honest woman,— 71

Escalus. Dost thou detest her therefore?

Elbow. I say, sir, I will detest myself also, as well as she, that this house, if it be not a bawd's house, it is pity of her life, for it is a naughty house.

Escalus. How dost thou know that, constable?

Elbow. Marry, sir, by my wife; who, if she had been a woman cardinally given, might have been accused in fornication, adultery, and all uncleanliness there.

Escalus. By the woman's means? 80

Elbow. Ay, sir, by Mistress Overdone's means; but as she spit in his face, so she defied him.

Pompey. Sir, if it please your honour, this is not so.

Elbow. Prove it before these varlets here, thou honourable man; prove it.

Escalus. Do you hear how he misplaces?

Pompey. Sir, she came in great with child, and longing, saving your honour's reverence, for stewed prunes; sir, we had but two in the house, which at that very distant time stood, as it were, in a fruit-dish, a dish of some three-pence : your honours have seen such dishes; they are not China dishes, but very good dishes,— 92

Escalus. Go to, go to; no matter for the dish, sir.

Pompey. No, indeed, sir, not of a pin; you are therein in the right : but to the point. As I say, this Mistress Elbow, being, as I say, with child, and being great-bellied, and longing, as I said, for prunes, and having but two in the dish, as I said, Master Froth here, this very man, having eaten the rest, as I said, and, as I say, paying for them very honestly,— for, as you know, Master Froth, I could not give you three-pence again. 101

Froth. No, indeed.

Pompey. Very well; you being then, if you be remembered, cracking the stones of the foresaid prunes,—

Froth. Ay, so I did indeed.

Pompey. Why, very well; I telling you then, if you be remembered, that such a one and such a one were past cure of the thing you wot of, unless they kept very good diet, as I told you,—

Froth. All this is true.   110

Pompey. Why, very well, then,—

Escalus. Come, you are a tedious fool; to the purpose. What was done to Elbow's wife, that he hath cause to complain of? Come me to what was done to her.

Pompey. Sir, your honour cannot come to that yet.

Escalus. No, sir, nor I mean it not.

Pompey. Sir, but you shall come to it, by your honour's leave. And, I beseech you, look into Master Froth here, sir; a man of fourscore pound a year, whose father died at Hallowmas.—Was 't not at Hallowmas, Master Froth?   120

Froth. All-hallownd eve.

Pompey. Why, very well; I hope here be truths. He, sir, sitting, as I say, in a lower chair, sir,—'t was in the Bunch of Grapes, where indeed you have a delight to sit, have you not?

Froth. I have so; because it is an open room and good for winter.

Pompey. Why, very well, then; I hope here be truths.

Angelo. This will last out a night in Russia,
When nights are longest there. I 'll take my leave,   130
And leave you to the hearing of the cause,
Hoping you 'll find good cause to whip them all.

Escalus. I think no less. Good morrow to your lordship.—   [*Exit Angelo.*

Now, sir, come on; what was done to Elbow's wife, once more?

Pompey. Once, sir? there was nothing done to her once.

Elbow. I beseech you, sir, ask him what this man did to my wife.

Pompey. I beseech your honour, ask me.

Escalus. Well, sir, what did this gentleman to her?   140

Pompey. I beseech you, sir, look in this gentleman's face.—Good Master Froth, look upon his honour; 't is for a good purpose.—Doth your honour mark his face?

Escalus. Ay, sir, very well.

Pompey. Nay, I beseech you, mark it well.

Escalus. Well, I do so.

Pompey. Doth your honour see any harm in his face?

Escalus. Why, no.

Pompey. I 'll be supposed upon a book, his face is the worst thing about him. Good, then; if his face be the worst thing about him, how could Master Froth do the constable's wife any harm? I would know that of your honour.   152

Escalus. He 's in the right. Constable, what say you to it?

Elbow. First, an it like you, the house is a respected house; next, this is a respected fellow, and his mistress is a respected woman.

Pompey. By this hand, sir, his wife is a more respected person than any of us all.

Elbow. Varlet, thou liest; thou liest, wicked varlet! the time is yet to come that she was ever respected with man, woman, or child.   162

Pompey. Sir, she was respected with him before he married with her.

Escalus. Which is the wiser here? Justice or Iniquity?—Is this true?

Elbow. O thou caitiff! O thou varlet! O thou wicked Hannibal! I respected with her before I was married to her!—If ever I was respected with her, or she with me, let not your worship think me the poor duke's officer.—Prove

this, thou wicked Hannibal, or I 'll have mine action of bat-
tery on thee.   172

Escalus. If he took you a box o' the ear, you might have
your action of slander too.

Elbow. Marry, I thank your good worship for it. What
is 't your worship's pleasure I shall do with this wicked
caitiff?

Escalus. Truly, officer, because he hath some offences in
him that thou wouldst discover if thou couldst, let him continue in his courses till thou knowest what they are.   180

Elbow. Marry, I thank your worship for it.—Thou seest,
thou wicked varlet, now, what 's come upon thee : thou art
to continue now, thou varlet ; thou art to continue.

Escalus. Where were you born, friend?

Froth. Here in Vienna, sir.

Escalus. Are you of fourscore pounds a year?

Froth. Yes, an 't please you, sir.

Escalus. So.—What trade are you of, sir?

Pompey. A tapster ; a poor widow's tapster.

Escalus. Your mistress' name?   190

Pompey. Mistress Overdone.

Escalus. Hath she had any more than one husband?

Pompey. Nine, sir ; Overdone by the last.

Escalus. Nine!—Come hither to me, Master Froth. Master Froth, I would not have you acquainted with tapsters ;
they will draw you, Master Froth, and you will hang them.
Get you gone, and let me hear no more of you.

Froth. I thank your worship. For mine own part, I never
come into any room in a taphouse, but I am drawn in.   199

Escalus. Well, no more of it, Master Froth : farewell.—
[*Exit Froth.*] Come you hither to me, Master Tapster.
What 's your name, Master Tapster?

Pompey. Pompey.

Escalus. What else?

Pompey. Bum, sir.

Escalus. Troth, and your bum is the greatest thing about
you ; so that in the beastliest sense you are Pompey the
Great. Pompey, you are partly a bawd, Pompey, howsoever
you colour it in being a tapster, are you not? come, tell me
true; it shall be the better for you.   210

Pompey. Truly, sir, I am a poor fellow that would live.

Escalus. How would you live, Pompey? by being a bawd?
What do you think of the trade, Pompey? is it a lawful
trade?

Pompey. If the law would allow it, sir.

Escalus. But the law will not allow it, Pompey ; nor it
shall not be allowed in Vienna.

Pompey. Does your worship mean to geld and spay all
the youth of the city?

Escalus. No, Pompey.   220

Pompey. Truly, sir, in my poor opinion, they will to 't then.
If your worship will take order for the drabs and the knaves,
you need not to fear the bawds.

Escalus. There are pretty orders beginning, I can tell you ;
it is but heading and hanging.

Pompey. If you head and hang all that offend that way but
for ten year together, you 'll be glad to give out a commission
for more heads. If this law hold in Vienna ten year, I 'll
rent the fairest house in it after three-pence a day. If you
live to see this come to pass, say Pompey told you so.   230

Escalus. Thank you, good Pompey ; and, in requital of your
prophecy, hark you : I advise you, let me not find you before
me again upon any complaint whatsoever; no, not for dwell-
ing where you do. If I do, Pompey, I shall beat you to your
tent, and prove a shrewd Cæsar to you; in plain dealing,
Pompey, I shall have you whipt. So, for this time, Pompey,
fare you well.

Pompey. I thank your worship for your good counsel ;
[*Aside*] but I shall follow it as the flesh and fortune shall
better determine.   240

Whip me? No, no; let carman whip his jade;
The valiant heart is not whipt out of his trade. [*Exit.*

Escalus. Come hither to me, Master Elbow; come hither,
Master Constable. How long have you been in this place
of constable?

Elbow. Seven year and a half, sir.

Escalus. I thought, by your readiness in the office, you
had continued in it some time. You say, seven years together?

Elbow. And a half, sir.   250

Escalus. Alas, it hath been great pains to you. They do
you wrong to put you so oft upon 't. Are there not men in
your ward sufficient to serve it?

Elbow. Faith, sir, few of any wit in such matters. As they
are chosen, they are glad to choose me for them; I do it for
some piece of money, and go through with all.

Escalus. Look you bring me in the names of some six or
seven, the most sufficient of your parish.

Elbow. To your worship's house, sir?

Escalus. To my house. Fare you well.— [*Exit Elbow.*
What 's o'clock, think you?   261

Justice. Eleven, sir.

Escalus. I pray you home to dinner with me.

Justice. I humbly thank you.

Escalus. It grieves me for the death of Claudio;
But there 's no remedy.

Justice. Lord Angelo is severe.

Escalus.   It is but needful.
Mercy is not itself, that oft looks so;
Pardon is still the nurse of second woe.
But yet,—poor Claudio! There is no remedy.   270
Come, sir.   [*Exeunt.*

SCENE II.   *Another* **Room** *in the Same.*

Enter PROVOST *and a* Servant.

Servant. He 's hearing of a cause; he will come straight.
I 'll tell him of you.

Provost.   Pray you, do.—[*Exit Servant.*] I 'll know
His pleasure; may be he will relent.   Alas,
He hath but as offended in a dream!
All sects, all ages smack of this vice; and he
To die for 't!—

Enter ANGELO.

Angelo.   Now, what 's the matter, provost?

Provost. Is it your will Claudio shall die to-morrow?

Angelo. Did not I tell thee yea? hadst thou not order?
Why dost thou ask again?

Provost.   Lest I might be too rash.
Under your good correction, I have seen,   10
When, after execution, judgment hath
Repented o'er his doom.

Angelo.   Go to; let that be mine.
Do you your office, or give up your place,
And you shall well be spar'd.

Provost.   I crave your honour's pardon.
What shall be done, sir, with the groaning Juliet?
She 's very near her hour.

Angelo.   Dispose of her
To some more fitter place, and that with speed.

Re-enter Servant.

Servant. Here is the sister of the man condemn'd
Desires access to you.

Angelo.   Hath he a sister?

Provost. Ay, my good lord; a very virtuous maid,   20
And to be shortly of a sisterhood,
If not already.

Angelo. Well, let her be admitted.— [*Exit Servant.*
See you the fornicatress be remov'd:
Let her have needful but not lavish means;
There shall be order for 't.

Enter ISABELLA *and* LUCIO.

Provost. Save your honour!
Angelo. Stay a little while.—[*To Isabella*] You 're wel-
    come; what 's your will?
Isabella. I am a woful suitor to your honour,
Please but your honour hear me.
Angelo. Well, what 's your suit?
Isabella. There is a vice that most I do abhor,
And most desire should meet the blow of justice;   30
For which I would not plead, but that I must;
For which I must not plead, but that I am
At war 'twixt will and will not.
Angelo. Well, the matter?
Isabella. I have a brother is condemn'd to die;
I do beseech you, let it be his fault,
And not my brother.
Provost. [*Aside*] Heaven give thee moving graces!
Angelo. Condemn the fault, and not the actor of it?
Why, every fault 's condemn'd ere it be done.
Mine were the very cipher of a function,
To fine the faults whose fine stands in record,   40
And let go by the actor.
Isabella. O just but severe law!
I had a brother, then. Heaven keep your honour!
Lucio. [*Aside to Isabella*] Give 't not o'er so: to him again,
    entreat him;
Kneel down before him, hang upon his gown.
You are too cold; if you should need a pin,
You could not with more tame a tongue desire it.
To him, I say!

Isabella. Must he needs die?

Angelo.   Maiden, no remedy.

Isabella. Yes; I do think that you might pardon him,
And neither heaven nor man grieve at the mercy.   50

Angelo. I will not do 't.

Isabella.   But can you, if you would?

Angelo. Look, what I will not, that I cannot do.

Isabella. But might you do 't, and do the world no wrong,
If so your heart were touch'd with that remorse
As mine is to him?

Angelo.   He 's sentenc'd; 't is too late.

Lucio. [*Aside to Isabella*] You are too cold.

Isabella. Too late? why, no; I, that do speak a word,
May call it back again. Well believe this,
No ceremony that to great ones longs,
Not the king's crown, nor the deputed sword,   60
The marshal's truncheon, nor the judge's robe,
Become them with one half so good a grace
As mercy does.
If he had been as you and you as he,
You would have slipt like him; but he like you
Would not have been so stern.

Angelo.   Pray you, be gone.

Isabella. I would to heaven I had your potency,
And you were Isabel! should it then be thus?
No; I would tell what 't were to be a judge,
And what a prisoner.

Lucio. [*Aside to Isabella*] Ay, touch him; there 's the
        vein.   70

Angelo. Your brother is a forfeit of the law,
And you but waste your words.

Isabella.   Alas, alas!
Why, all the souls that were were forfeit once,
And He that might the vantage best have took
Found out the remedy. How would you be,

If He, which is the top of judgment, should
But judge you as you are?   O, think on that!
And mercy then will breathe within your lips,
Like man new made.
    Angelo.   Be you content, fair maid;
It is the law, not I condemn your brother.   80
Were he my kinsman, brother, or my son,
It should be thus with him; he must die to-morrow.
    Isabella. To - morrow!   O, that 's sudden!   Spare him,
        spare him!
He 's not prepar'd for death.   Even for our kitchens
We kill the fowl of season ; shall we serve heaven
With less respect than we do minister
To our gross selves?   Good, good my lord, bethink you ;
Who is it that hath died for this offence?
There 's many have committed it.
    Lucio.   [*Aside to Isabella*] Ay, well said.   89
    Angelo. The law hath not been dead, though it hath slept.
Those many had not dar'd to do that evil,
If the first that did the edict infringe
Had answer'd for his deed ; now 't is awake,
Takes note of what is done, and, like a prophet,
Looks in a glass, that shows what future evils,
Either new, or by remissness new-conceiv'd,
And so in progress to be hatch'd and born,
Are now to have no successive degrees,
But, ere they live, to end.
    Isabella.   Yet show some pity.
    Angelo. I show it most of all when I show justice ;   100
For then I pity those I do not know,
Which a dismiss'd offence would after gall,
And do him right that, answering one foul wrong,
Lives not to act another.   Be satisfied ;
Your brother dies to-morrow ; be content.
    Isabella. So you must be the first that gives this sentence,

And he that suffers.   O, it is excellent
To have a giant's strength, but it is tyrannous
To use it like a giant.
    Lucio. [*Aside to Isabella*] That 's well said.
    Isabella. Could great men thunder   110
As Jove himself does, Jove would ne'er be quiet,
For every pelting, petty officer
Would use his heaven for thunder;
Nothing but thunder!   Merciful Heaven,
Thou rather with thy sharp and sulphurous bolt
Split'st the unwedgeable and gnarled oak
Than the soft myrtle; but man, proud man,
Drest in a little brief authority,
Most ignorant of what he 's most assur'd,
His glassy essence, like an angry ape,   120
Plays such fantastic tricks before high heaven
As make the angels weep, who, with our spleens,
Would all themselves laugh mortal.
    Lucio. [*Aside to Isabella*] O, to him, to him, wench! he will
    relent:
He 's coming; I perceive 't.
    Provost.   [*Aside*] Pray heaven she win him!
    Isabella. We cannot weigh our brother with ourself.
Great men may jest with saints; 't is wit in them,
But in the less foul profanation.
    Lucio. Thou 'rt i' the right, girl; more o' that.
    Isabella. That in the captain 's but a choleric word   130
Which in the soldier is flat blasphemy.
    Lucio. [*Aside to Isabella*] Art avis'd o' that? more on 't.
    Angelo. Why do you put these sayings upon me?
    Isabella. Because authority, though it err like others,
Hath yet a kind of medicine in itself,
That skins the vice o' the top.   Go to your bosom;
Knock there, and ask your heart what it doth know
That 's like my brother's fault: if it confess

A natural guiltiness such as is his,
Let it not sound a thought upon your tongue   140
Against my brother's life.
    Angelo.   [*Aside*] She speaks, and 't is
Such sense, that my sense breeds with it.—Fare you well.
    Isabella. Gentle my lord, turn back.
    Angelo. I will bethink me ; come again to-morrow.
    Isabella. Hark how I 'll bribe you ; good my lord, turn
        back.
    Angelo. How ! bribe me ?
    Isabella. Ay, with such gifts that heaven shall share with
        you.
    Lucio. [*Aside to Isabella*] You had marr'd all else.
    Isabella. Not with fond shekels of the tested gold,
Or stones whose rates are either rich or poor   150
As fancy values them, but with true prayers
That shall be up at heaven and enter there
Ere sunrise, prayers from preserved souls,
From fasting maids whose minds are dedicate
To nothing temporal.
    Angelo.   Well ; come to me to-morrow.
    Lucio. [*Aside to Isabella*] Go to ; 't is well ; away !
    Isabella. Heaven keep your honour safe !
    Angelo.   [*Aside*] Amen ;
For I am that way going to temptation,
Where prayers cross.
    Isabella.   At what hour to-morrow
Shall I attend your lordship ?
    Angelo.   At any time fore noon.   160
    Isabella. Save your honour !
                    [*Exeunt Isabella, Lucio, and Provost.*
    Angelo.   From thee,—even from thy virtue !
What 's this, what 's this ? Is this her fault or mine ?
The tempter or the tempted, who sins most ? Ha !
Not she ; nor doth she tempt : but it is I
                    E

That, lying by the violet in the sun,
Do as the carrion does, not as the flower,
Corrupt with virtuous season.   Can it be
That modesty may more betray our sense
Than woman's lightness?   Having waste ground enough,
Shall we desire to raze the sanctuary   170
And pitch our evils there?   O, fie, fie, fie!
What dost thou, or what art thou, Angelo?
Dost thou desire her foully for those things
That make her good?   O, let her brother live!
Thieves for their robbery have authority
When judges steal themselves.   What! do I love her,
That I desire to hear her speak again,
And feast upon her eyes?   What is 't I dream on?
O cunning enemy, that, to catch a saint,
With saints dost bait thy hook!   Most dangerous   180
Is that temptation that doth goad us on
To sin in loving virtue.   Never could the strumpet,
With all her double vigour, art and nature,
Once stir my temper, but this virtuous maid
Subdues me quite.   Ever till now,
When men were fond, I smil'd and wonder'd how.   [*Exit.*

SCENE III.   *A Room in a Prison.*

Enter, severally, DUKE, *disguised as a friar, and* PROVOST.

Duke. Hail to you, provost!—so I think you are.
Provost. I am the provost.   What 's your will, good friar?
Duke. Bound by my charity and my blest order,
I come to visit the afflicted spirits
Here in the prison.   Do me the common right
To let me see them and to make me know
The nature of their crimes, that I may minister
To them accordingly.
Provost. I would do more than that, if more were needful.

Enter JULIET.

Look, here comes one ; a gentlewoman of mine,   10
Who, falling in the flames of her own youth,
Hath blister'd her report.   She is with child ;
And he that got it, sentenced—a young man
More fit to do another such offence
Than die for this.
  Duke. When must he die?
  Provost.   As I do think, to-morrow.—
[*To Juliet*] I have provided for you ; stay awhile,
And you shall be conducted.
  Duke. Repent you, fair one, of the sin you carry?   ·
  Juliet. I do, and bear the shame most patiently.   20
  Duke. I 'll teach you how you shall arraign your con-
      science,
And try your penitence, if it be sound,
Or hollowly put on.
  Juliet.   I 'll gladly learn.
  Duke. Love you the man that wrong'd you?
  Juliet. Yes, as I love the woman that wrong'd him.
  Duke. So then it seems your most offenceful act
Was mutually committed?
  Juliet.   Mutually.
  Duke. Then was your sin of heavier kind than his.
  Juliet. I do confess it, and repent it, father.
  Duke. 'T is meet so, daughter ; but lest you do repent, 30
As that the sin hath brought you to this shame,
Which sorrow is always towards ourselves, not heaven,
Showing we would not spare heaven as we love it,
But as we stand in fear,—
  Juliet. I do repent me, as it is an evil,
And take the shame with joy.
  Duke.   There rest.
Your partner, as I hear, must die to-morrow,

And I am going with instruction to him.
Grace go with you! Benedicite!   [*Exit.*
    Juliet. Must die to-morrow! O injurious law,   40
That respites me a life, whose very comfort
Is still a dying horror!
    Provost.   'T is pity of him.   [*Exeunt.*

SCENE IV. *A Room in* ANGELO'S *House.*

Enter ANGELO.

    Angelo. When I would pray and think, I think and pray
To several subjects. Heaven hath my empty words,
Whilst my invention, hearing not my tongue,
Anchors on Isabel; Heaven in my mouth,
As if I did but only chew his name,
And in my heart the strong and swelling evil
Of my conception. The state whereon I studied,
Is like a good thing, being often read,
Grown sear'd and tedious; yea, my gravity,
Wherein—let no man hear me—I take pride,   10
Could I with boot change for an idle plume,
Which the air beats for vain. O place, O form,
How often dost thou with thy case, thy habit,
Wrench awe from fools and tie the wiser souls
To thy false seeming! Blood, thou art blood;
Let 's write good angel on the devil's horn,
'T is not the devil's crest.—

Enter a Servant.

                    How now! who 's there?
    Servant. One Isabel, a sister, desires access to you.
    Angelo. Teach her the way.—[*Exit Servant.*] O heavens!
Why does my blood thus muster to my heart,   20
Making both it unable for itself,
And dispossessing all my other parts
Of necessary fitness?

So play the foolish throngs with one that swoons,—
Come all to help him, and so stop the air
By which he should revive ; and even so
The general, subject to a well-wish'd king,
Quit their own part, and in obsequious fondness
Crowd to his presence, where their untaught love
Must needs appear offence.—

Enter ISABELLA.

How now, fair maid?   30
Isabella. I am come to know your pleasure.
Angelo. That you might know it, would much better please
   me
Than to demand what 't is.   Your brother cannot live.
Isabella. Even so.—Heaven keep your honour !
Angelo. Yet may he live awhile, and, it may be,
As long as you or I ; yet he must die.
Isabella. Under your sentence ?
Angelo. Yea.
Isabella. When, I beseech you ? that in his reprieve,
Longer or shorter, he may be so fitted   40
That his soul sicken not.
   Angelo. Ha ! fie, these filthy vices !   It were as good
To pardon him that hath from nature stolen
A man already made, as to remit
Their saucy sweetness that do coin heaven's image
In stamps that are forbid ; 't is all as easy
Falsely to take away a life true made
As to put metal in restrained means
To make a false one.
   Isabella. 'T is set down so in heaven, but not in earth.   50
   Angelo. Say you so ? then I shall pose you quickly.
Which had you rather, that the most just law
Now took your brother's life, or, to redeem him,
Give up your body to such sweet uncleanness
As she that he hath stain'd?

Isabella.   Sir, believe this,
I had rather give my body than my soul.

Angelo. I talk not of your soul ; our compell'd sins
Stand more for number than for accompt.

Isabella.   How say you?

Angelo. Nay, I 'll not warrant that; for I can speak
Against the thing I say.   Answer to this :   60
I, now the voice of the recorded law,
Pronounce a sentence on your brother's life ;
Might there not be a charity in sin
To save this brother's life?

Isabella.   Please you to do 't,
I 'll take it as a peril to my soul,
It is no sin at all, but charity.

Angelo. Pleas'd you to do 't at peril of your soul,
Were equal poise of sin and charity.

Isabella. That I do beg his life, if it be sin,
Heaven let me bear it! you granting of my suit,   70
If that be sin, I 'll make it my morn prayer
To have it added to the faults of mine,
And nothing of your answer.

Angelo.   Nay, but hear me.
Your sense pursues not mine ; either you are ignorant,
Or seem so craftily, and that 's not good.

Isabella. Let me be ignorant, and in nothing good,
But graciously to know I am no better.

Angelo. Thus wisdom wishes to appear most bright,
When it doth tax itself ; as these black masks
Proclaim an enshield beauty ten times louder   80
Than beauty could, display'd.   But mark me ;
To be received plain, I 'll speak more gross.
Your brother is to die.

Isabella. So.

Angelo. And his offence is so, as it appears
Accountant to the law upon that pain.

Isabella. True.

Angelo. Admit no other way to save his life,—
As I subscribe not that, nor any other,
But in the loss of question,—that you, his sister,   90
Finding yourself desir'd of such a person,
Whose credit with the judge, or own great place,
Could fetch your brother from the manacles
Of the all-holding law, and that there were
No earthly mean to save him, but that either
You must lay down the treasures of your body
To this suppos'd, or else to let him suffer,
What would you do?

Isabella. As much for my poor brother as myself:
That is, were I under the terms of death,   100
The impression of keen whips I 'd wear as rubies,
And strip myself to death, as to a bed
That longing I 've been sick for, ere I 'd yield
My body up to shame.

Angelo.   Then must your brother die.

Isabella. And 't were the cheaper way.
Better it were a brother died at once,
Than that a sister, by redeeming him,
Should die for ever.

Angelo. Were not you then as cruel as the sentence
That you have slander'd so?   110

Isabella. Ignomy in ransom and free pardon
Are of two houses; lawful mercy
Is nothing kin to foul redemption.

Angelo. You seem'd of late to make the law a tyrant,
And rather prov'd the sliding of your brother
A merriment than a vice.

Isabella. O, pardon me, my lord; it oft falls out,
To have what we would have, we speak not what we mean.
I something do excuse the thing I hate,
For his advantage that I dearly love.   120

Angelo. We are all frail.

Isabella.   Else let my brother die,
If not a fedary but only he
Owe and succeed thy weakness.

Angelo. Nay, women are frail too.

Isabella. Ay, as the glasses where they view themselves,
Which are as easy broke as they make forms.
Women! Help Heaven! men their creation mar
In profiting by them. Nay, call us ten times frail;
For we are soft as our complexions are,
And credulous to false prints.

Angelo.   I think it well;   130
And from this testimony of your own sex,—
Since I suppose we are made to be no stronger
Than faults may shake our frames,—let me be bold;
I do arrest your words. Be that you are,
That is, a woman; if you be more, you 're none;
If you be one, as you are well express'd
By all external warrants, show it now,
By putting on the destin'd livery.

Isabella. I have no tongue but one; gentle my lord,
Let me entreat you speak the former language.   140

Angelo. Plainly conceive, I love you.

Isabella. My brother did love Juliet,
And you tell me that he shall die for it.

Angelo. He shall not, Isabel, if you give me love.

Isabella. I know your virtue hath a license in 't,
Which seems a little fouler than it is,
To pluck on others.

Angelo.   Believe me, on mine honour,
My words express my purpose.

Isabella. Ha! little honour to be much believ'd,
And most pernicious purpose! Seeming, seeming!   150
I will proclaim thee, Angelo; look for 't!
Sign me a present pardon for my brother,

Or with an outstretch'd throat I 'll tell the world aloud
What man thou art.
   Angelo.   Who will believe thee, Isabel?
My unsoil'd name, the austereness of my life,
My vouch against you, and my place i' the state,
Will so your accusation overweigh,
That you shall stifle in your own report
And smell of calumny. I have begun,
And now I give my sensual race the rein: 160
Fit thy consent to my sharp appetite;
Lay by all nicety and prolixious blushes,
That banish what they sue for; redeem thy brother
By yielding up thy body to my will,
Or else he must not only die the death,
But thy unkindness shall his death draw out
To lingering sufferance. Answer me to-morrow,
Or, by the affection that now guides me most,
I 'll prove a tyrant to him. As for you,   169
Say what you can, my false o'erweighs your true.   [*Exit.*
   Isabella. To whom should I complain? Did I tell this,
Who would believe me? O perilous mouths,
That bear in them one and the self-same tongue,
Either of condemnation or approof;
Bidding the law make court'sy to their will,
Hooking both right and wrong to the appetite,
To follow as it draws! I 'll to my brother.
Though he hath fall'n by prompture of the blood,
Yet hath he in him such a mind of honour,
That, had he twenty heads to tender down   180
On twenty bloody blocks, he 'd yield them up,
Before his sister should her body stoop
To such abhorr'd pollution.
Then, Isabel, live chaste, and, brother, die;
More than our brother is our chastity.
I 'll tell him yet of Angelo's request,
And fit his mind to death, for his soul's rest.   [*Exit.*

STREET BEFORE THE PRISON (SCENE II.).

ACT III.

SCENE I.   *A Room in the Prison.*

Enter DUKE *disguised as before,* CLAUDIO, *and* PROVOST.

Duke. So then you hope of pardon from Lord Angelo?

Claudio. The miserable have no other medicine

But only hope.
I 've hope to live, and am prepar'd to die.
  Duke. Be absolute for death ; either death or life
Shall thereby be the sweeter. Reason thus with life :
If I do lose thee, I do lose a thing
That none but fools would keep ; a breath thou art,
Servile to all the skyey influences,
That dost this habitation where thou keep'st   10
Hourly afflict. Merely, thou art death's fool ;
For him thou labour'st by thy flight to shun,
And yet runn'st toward him still. Thou art not noble ;
For all the accommodations that thou bear'st
Are nurs'd by baseness. Thou 'rt by no means valiant ;
For thou dost fear the soft and tender fork
Of a poor worm. Thy best of rest is sleep,
And that thou oft provok'st ; yet grossly fear'st
Thy death, which is no more. Thou art not thyself ;
For thou exist'st on many a thousand grains   20
That issue out of dust. Happy thou art not ;
For what thou hast not, still thou striv'st to get,
And what thou hast, forget'st. Thou art not certain ;
For thy complexion shifts to strange effects,
After the moon. If thou art rich, thou 'rt poor ;
For, like an ass whose back with ingots bows,
Thou bear'st thy heavy riches but a journey,
And death unloads thee. Friend hast thou none ;
For thine own bowels, which do call thee sire,
The mere effusion of thy proper loins,   30
Do curse the gout, serpigo, and the rheum,
For ending thee no sooner. Thou hast nor youth nor age,
But, as it were, an after-dinner's sleep,
Dreaming on both ; for all thy blessed youth
Becomes as aged, and doth beg the alms
Of palsied eld ; and when thou art old and rich,
Thou hast neither heat, affection, limb, nor beauty,

To make thy riches pleasant.   What 's yet in this
That bears the name of life?   Yet in this life
Lie hid moe thousand deaths; yet death we fear,   40
That makes these odds all even.
    Claudio.   I humbly thank you.
To sue to live, I find I seek to die,
And, seeking death, find life; let it come on.
    Isabella. [*Within*] What, ho!   Peace here; grace and
        good company!
    Provost. Who 's there? come in; the wish deserves a wel-
        come.
    Duke. Dear sir, ere long I 'll visit you again.
    Claudio. Most holy sir, I thank you.

                    Enter ISABELLA.

    Isabella. My business is a word or two with Claudio.
    Provost. And very welcome.—Look, signior, here 's your
        sister.
    Duke. Provost, a word with you.   50
    Provost. As many as you please.
    Duke. Bring me to hear them speak, where I may be con-
cealed.   [*Exeunt Duke and Provost.*
    Claudio. Now, sister, what 's the comfort?
    Isabella.   Why?
As all comforts are; most good, most good indeed.
Lord Angelo, having affairs to heaven,
Intends you for his swift ambassador,
Where you shall be an everlasting lieger.
Therefore your best appointment make with speed;
To-morrow you set on.
    Claudio.   Is there no remedy?   60
    Isabella. None, but such remedy as, to save a head,
To cleave a heart in twain.
    Claudio.   But is there any?
    Isabella. Yes, brother, you may live;

There is a devilish mercy in the judge,
If you 'll implore it, that will free your life,
But fetter you till death.
    Claudio.   Perpetual durance?
    Isabella. Ay, just; perpetual durance, a restraint,
Though all the world's vastidity you had,
To a determin'd scope.
    Claudio.   But in what nature?
    Isabella. In such a one as, you consenting to 't,   .   70
Would bark your honour from that trunk you bear,
And leave you naked.
    Claudio.   Let me know the point.
    Isabella. O, I do fear thee, Claudio; and I quake,
Lest thou a feverous life shouldst entertain,
And six or seven winters more respect
Than a perpetual honour. Dar'st thou die?
The sense of death is most in apprehension;
And the poor beetle, that we tread upon,
In corporal sufferance finds a pang as great
As when a giant dies.
    Claudio.   Why give you me this shame?   80
Think you I can a resolution fetch
From flowery tenderness? If I must die,
I will encounter darkness as a bride,
And hug it in mine arms.
    Isabella. There spake my brother; there my father's grave
Did utter forth a voice. Yes, thou must die;
Thou art too noble to conserve a life
In base appliances. This outward-sainted deputy,
Whose settled visage and deliberate word
Nips youth i' the head, and follies doth emmew   90
As falcon doth the fowl, is yet a devil;
His filth within being cast, he would appear
A pond as deep as hell.
    Claudio.   The priestly Angelo!

Isabella. O, 't is the cunning livery of hell,
The damned'st body to invest and cover
In priestly guards! Dost thou think, Claudio?
If I would yield him my virginity,
Thou mightst be freed.
    Claudio.   O heavens! it cannot be.
    Isabella. Yes, he would give 't thee, from this rank of-
    fence,
So to offend him still. This night 's the time   100
That I should do what I abhor to name,
Or else thou diest to-morrow.
    Claudio.   Thou shalt not do 't.
    Isabella. O, were it but my life,
I 'd throw it down for your deliverance
As frankly as a pin.
    Claudio.   .   Thanks, dear Isabel.
    Isabella. Be ready, Claudio, for your death to-morrow.
    Claudio. Yes. Has he affections in him,
That thus can make him bite the law by the nose,
When he would force it? Sure, it is no sin;
Or of the deadly seven it is the least.   110
    Isabella. Which is the least?
    Claudio. If it were damnable, he being so wise,
Why would he for the momentary trick
Be perdurably fin'd?—O Isabel!
    Isabella. What says my brother?
    Claudio.   Death is a fearful thing
    Isabella. And shamed life a hateful.
    Claudio. Ay, but to die, and go we know not where;
To lie in cold obstruction and to rot;
This sensible warm motion to become
A kneaded clod; and the delighted spirit   120
To bathe in fiery floods, or to reside
In thrilling region of thick-ribbed ice;
To be imprison'd in the viewless winds,

And blown with restless violence round about
The pendent world; or to be worse than worst
Of those that lawless and incertain thought
Imagine howling!—'t is too horrible!
The weariest and most loathed worldly life
That age, ache, penury, and imprisonment
Can lay on nature is a paradise   13c
To what we fear of death.
 Isabella. Alas, alas!
 Claudio.   Sweet sister, let me live.
What sin you do to save a brother's life,
Nature dispenses with the deed so far
That it becomes a virtue.
 Isabella.   O you beast!
O faithless coward! O dishonest wretch!
Wilt thou be made a man out of my vice?
Is 't not a kind of incest to take life
From thine own sister's shame? What should I think?
Heaven shield my mother play'd my father fair!   140
For such a warped slip of wilderness
Ne'er issued from his blood. Take my defiance!
Die, perish! Might but my bending down
Reprieve thee from thy fate, it should proceed.
I'll pray a thousand prayers for thy death,
No word to save thee.
 Claudio. Nay, hear me, Isabel.
 Isabella.   O, fie, fie, fie!
Thy sin's not accidental, but a trade.
Mercy to thee would prove itself a bawd;
'T is best that thou diest quickly.
 Claudio.   O hear me, Isabella!   150

Re-enter DUKE.

 Duke. Vouchsafe a word, young sister, but one word.
 Isabella. What is your will?

Duke. Might you dispense with your leisure, I would by and by have some speech with you; the satisfaction I would require is likewise your own benefit.   155

Isabella. I have no superfluous leisure : my stay must be stolen out of other affairs; but I will attend you awhile.

[*Walks apart.*

Duke. Son, I have overheard what hath passed between you and your sister. Angelo had never the purpose to corrupt her ; only he hath made an assay of her virtue to practise his judgment with the disposition of natures. She, having the truth of honour in her, hath made him that gracious denial which he is most glad to receive. I am confessor to Angelo, and I know this to be true ; therefore prepare yourself to death. Do not satisfy your resolution with hopes that are fallible : to-morrow you must die ; go to your knees and make ready.

Claudio. Let me ask my sister pardon. I am so out of love with life that I will sue to be rid of it.   169

Duke. Hold you there ; farewell.—[*Exit Claudio.*] Provost, a word with you !

Re-enter PROVOST.

Provost. What's your will, father ?

Duke. That now you are come, you will be gone. Leave me awhile with the maid ; my mind promises with my habit no loss shall touch her by my company.

Provost. In good time.

[*Exit Provost. Isabella comes forward.*

Duke. The hand that hath made you fair hath made you good : the goodness that is cheap in beauty makes beauty brief in goodness ; but grace, being the soul of your complexion, shall keep the body of it ever fair. The assault that Angelo hath made to you, fortune hath conveyed to my understanding ; and, but that frailty hath examples for his falling, I should wonder at Angelo. How will you do to content this substitute, and to save your brother ?   181

Isabella. I am now going to resolve him. I had rather my brother die by the law than my son should be unlawfully born. But, O, how much is the good duke deceived in Angelo! If ever he return, and I can speak to him, I will open my lips in vain, or discover his government. 189

Duke. That shall not be much amiss : yet, as the matter now stands, he will avoid your accusation ; he made trial of you only. Therefore fasten your ear on my advisings : to the love I have in doing good a remedy presents itself. I do make myself believe that you may most uprighteously do a poor wronged lady a merited benefit, redeem your brother from the angry law, do no stain to your own gracious person, and much please the absent duke, if peradventure he shall ever return to have hearing of this business.

Isabella. Let me hear you speak farther. I have spirit to do any thing that appears not foul in the truth of my spirit.

Duke. Virtue is bold, and goodness never fearful. Have you not heard speak of Mariana, the sister of Frederick the great soldier who miscarried at sea ? 203

Isabella. I have heard of the lady, and good words went with her name.

Duke. She should this Angelo have married ; was affianced to her by oath, and the nuptial appointed : between which time of the contract and limit of the solemnity, her brother Frederick was wracked at sea, having in that perished vessel the dowry of his sister. But mark how heavily this befell to the poor gentlewoman : there she lost a noble and renowned brother, in his love toward her ever most kind and natural; with him, the portion and sinew of her fortune, her marriage-dowry ; with both, her combinate husband, this well-seeming Angelo. 215

Isabella. Can this be so ? did Angelo so leave her ?

Duke. Left her in her tears, and dried not one of them with his comfort ; swallowed his vows whole, pretending in her discoveries of dishonour : in few, bestowed her on her own

F

lamentation, which she yet wears for his sake, and he, a marble to her tears, is washed with them, but relents not.

Isabella. What a merit were it in death to take this poor maid from the world! What corruption in this life, that it will let this man live! But how out of this can she avail?

Duke. It is a rupture that you may easily heal; and the cure of it not only saves your brother, but keeps you from dishonour in doing it.

Isabella. Show me how, good father.   228

Duke. This forenamed maid hath yet in her the continuance of her first affection; his unjust unkindness, that in all reason should have quenched her love, hath, like an impediment in the current, made it more violent and unruly. Go you to Angelo; answer his requiring with a plausible obedience; agree with his demands to the point; only refer yourself to this advantage, first, that your stay with him may not be long, that the time may have all shadow and silence in it, and the place answer to convenience. This being granted in course—and now follows all—we shall advise this wronged maid to stead up your appointment, go in your place; if the encounter acknowledge itself hereafter, it may compel him to her recompense: and here, by this, is your brother saved, your honour untainted, the poor Mariana advantaged, and the corrupt deputy foiled. The maid will I frame and make fit for his attempt. If you think well to carry this as you may, the doubleness of the benefit defends the deceit from reproof. What think you of it?   246

Isabella. The image of it gives me content already, and I trust it will grow to a most prosperous perfection.

Duke. It lies much in your holding up. Haste you speedily to Angelo; if for this night he entreat you to his bed, give him promise of satisfaction. I will presently to Saint Luke's; there, at the moated grange, resides this dejected Mariana. At that place call upon me, and dispatch with Angelo, that it may be quickly.

Isabella. I thank you for this comfort. Fare you well, good father. [*Exeunt severally.*

SCENE II. *The Street before the Prison.*

Enter, on one side, DUKE *disguised as before; on the other,* ELBOW, *and* Officers *with* POMPEY.

Elbow. Nay, if there be no remedy for it, but that you will needs buy and sell men and women like beasts, we shall have all the world drink brown and white bastard.

Duke. O heavens! what stuff is here?

Pompey. 'T was never merry world since, of two usuries, the merriest was put down, and the worser allowed by order of law a furred gown to keep him warm; and furred with fox and lamb skins too, to signify that craft, being richer than innocency, stands for the facing. 9

Elbow. Come your way, sir.—Bless you, good father friar.

Duke. And you, good brother father. What offence hath this man made you, sir?

Elbow. Marry, sir, he hath offended the law; and, sir, we take him to be a thief too, sir, for we have found upon him, sir, a strange picklock, which we have sent to the deputy.

Duke. Fie, sirrah! a bawd, a wicked bawd!
The evil that thou causest to be done,
That is thy means to live. Do thou but think
What 't is to cram a maw or clothe a back
From such a filthy vice; say to thyself, 20
From their abominable and beastly touches
I drink, I eat, array myself, and live.
Canst thou believe thy living is a life,
So stinkingly depending? Go mend, go mend.

Pompey. Indeed, it does stink in some sort, sir; but, yet, sir, I would prove—

Duke. Nay, if the devil have given thee proofs for sin,
Thou wilt prove his.—Take him to prison, officer.

Correction and instruction must both work
Ere this rude beast will profit.   30
Elbow. He must before the deputy, sir ; he has given him
warning. The deputy cannot abide a whoremaster ; if he be
a whoremonger, and comes before him, he were as good go
a mile on his errand.
Duke. That we were all, as some would seem to be,
Free from our faults, as from faults seeming free !
Elbow. His neck will come to your waist,—a cord, sir.
Pompey. I spy comfort ; I cry bail. Here 's a gentleman
and a friend of mine.   39

Enter LUCIO.

Lucio. How now, noble Pompey ! What, at the wheels of
Cæsar ? art thou led in triumph ? What, is there none of
Pygmalion's images, newly made woman, to be had now, for
putting the hand in the pocket and extracting it clutched ?
What reply, ha ? What sayest thou to this tune, matter, and
method ? Is 't not drowned i' the last rain, ha ? What sayest thou, Trot ? Is the world as it was, man ? Which is the
way ? Is it sad, and few words ? or how ? The trick of it ?
Duke. Still thus, and thus ; still worse !
Lucio. How doth my dear morsel, thy mistress ? Procures
she still, ha ?   50
Pompey. Troth, sir, she hath eaten up all her beef, and she
is herself in the tub.
Lucio. Why, 't is good ; it is the right of it ; it must be so :
an unshunned consequence ; it must be so. Art going to
prison, Pompey ?
Pompey. Yes, faith, sir.
Lucio. Why, 't is not amiss, Pompey. Farewell ; go, say I
sent thee thither. For debt, Pompey ? or how ?
Elbow. For being a bawd, for being a bawd.   59
Lucio. Well, then, imprison him. If imprisonment be the
due of a bawd, why, 't is his right ; bawd is he doubtless, and

of antiquity too—bawd-born. Farewell, good Pompey. Commend me to the prison, Pompey. You will turn good husband now, Pompey ; you will keep the house.

Pompey. I hope, sir, your good worship will be my bail.

Lucio. No, indeed, will I not, Pompey; it is not the wear.
I will pray, Pompey, to increase your bondage ; if you take
it not patiently, why, your mettle is the more. Adieu, trusty
Pompey.—Bless you, friar.

Duke. And you.   70

Lucio. Does Bridget paint still, Pompey, ah?

Elbow. Come your ways, sir ; come.

Pompey. You will not bail me, then, sir ?

Lucio. Then, Pompey, nor now.—What news abroad,
friar? what news?

Elbow. Come your ways, sir; come.

Lucio. Go to kennel, Pompey, go.—[*Exeunt Elbow, Pompey and Officers.*]   What news, friar, of the duke ?

Duke. I know none. Can you tell me of any?

Lucio. Some say he is with the Emperor of Russia ; other
some, he is in Rome; but where is he, think you?   81

Duke. I know not where ; but wheresoever, I wish him
well.

Lucio. It was a mad fantastical trick of him to steal from
the state, and usurp the beggary he was never born to. Lord
Angelo dukes it well in his absence ; he puts transgression
to 't.

Duke. He does well in 't.

Lucio. A little more lenity to lechery would do no harm in
him ; something too crabbed that way, friar.   90

Duke. It is too general a vice, and severity must cure it.

Lucio. Yes, in good sooth, the vice is of a great kindred ;
it is well allied : but it is impossible to extirp it quite, friar,
till eating and drinking be put down. They say this Angelo
was not made by man and woman after this downright way
of creation ; is it true, think you?

Duke. How should he be made, then?

Lucio. Some report a sea-maid spawned him; some, that he was begot between two stock-fishes.

Duke. You are pleasant, sir, and speak apace.   100

Lucio. Why, what a ruthless thing is this in him, for the rebellion of a codpiece to take away the life of a man! Would the duke that is absent have done this? Ere he would have hanged a man for the getting a hundred bastards, he would have paid for the nursing a thousand. He had some feeling of the sport; he knew the service, and that instructed him to mercy.

Duke. I never heard the absent duke much detected for women; he was not inclined that way.

Lucio. O, sir, you are deceived.   110

Duke. 'T is not possible.

Lucio. Who, not the duke? yes, your beggar of fifty; and his use was to put a ducat in her clack-dish: the duke had crotchets in him. He would be drunk too; that let me inform you.

Duke. You do him wrong, surely.

Lucio. Sir, I was an inward of his. A shy fellow was the duke; and I believe I know the cause of his withdrawing.

Duke. What, I prithee, might be the cause?   119

Lucio. No, pardon; 't is a secret must be locked within the teeth and the lips: but this I can let you understand, the greater file of the subject held the duke to be wise.

Duke. Wise! why, no question but he was.

Lucio. A very superficial, ignorant, unweighing fellow.

Duke. Either this is envy in you, folly, or mistaking; the very stream of his life and the business he hath helmed must upon a warranted need give him a better proclamation. Let him be but testimonied in his own bringings-forth, and he shall appear to the envious a scholar, a statesman, and a soldier. Therefore you speak unskilfully; or if your knowledge be more, it is much darkened in your malice.   131

Lucio. Sir, I know him, and I love him.

Duke. Love talks with better knowledge, and knowledge with dearer love.

Lucio. Come, sir, I know what I know.

Duke. I can hardly believe that, since you know not what you speak. But, if ever the duke return, as our prayers are he may, let me desire you to make your answer before him. If it be honest you have spoke, you have courage to maintain it. I am bound to call upon you; and, I pray you, your name? 141

Lucio. Sir, my name is Lucio, well known to the duke.

Duke. He shall know you better, sir, if I may live to report you.

Lucio. I fear you not.

Duke. O, you hope the duke will return no more, or you imagine me too unhurtful an opposite. But indeed I can do you little harm; you 'll forswear this again.

Lucio. I 'll be hanged first; thou art deceived in me, friar. But no more of this. Canst thou tell if Claudio die to-morrow or no? 151

Duke. Why should he die, sir?

Lucio. Why? For filling a bottle with a tun-dish. I would the duke we talk of were returned again: this ungenitured agent will unpeople the province with continency; sparrows must not build in his house-eaves, because they are lecherous. The duke yet would have dark deeds darkly answered; he would never bring them to light: would he were returned! Marry, this Claudio is condemned for untrussing. Farewell, good friar; I prithee, pray for me. The duke, I say to thee again, would eat mutton on Fridays. He 's not past it yet, and I say to thee, he would mouth with a beggar, though she smelt brown bread and garlic; say that I said so. Farewell. [*Exit.*

Duke. No might nor greatness in mortality 165
Can censure scape; back-wounding calumny

The whitest virtue strikes.   What king so strong
Can tie the gall up in the slanderous tongue?—
But who comes here?

Enter ESCALUS, PROVOST, *and* Officers *with* MISTRESS OVER-
DONE.

Escalus. Go; away with her to prison!   170
Mrs. Overdone. Good my lord, be good to me; your honour is accounted a merciful man, good my lord.
Escalus. Double and treble admonition, and still forfeit
in the same kind!   This would make mercy swear and play
the tyrant.
Provost. A bawd of eleven years' continuance, may it
please your honour.
Mrs. Overdone. My lord, this is one Lucio's information
against me.   Mistress Kate Keepdown was with child by him
in the duke's time; he promised her marriage: his child
is a year and a quarter old, come Philip and Jacob.   I have
kept it myself; and see how he goes about to abuse me!
Escalus. That fellow is a fellow of much license;—let him
be called before us.—Away with her to prison!—Go to;
no more words.—[*Exeunt Officers with Mistress Overdone.*]
Provost, my brother Angelo will not be altered; Claudio
must die to-morrow.   Let him be furnished with divines, and
have all charitable preparation.   If my brother wrought by
my pity, it should not be so with him.
Provost. So please you, this friar hath been with him, and
advised him for the entertainment of death.   191
Escalus. Good even, good father.
Duke. Bliss and goodness on you!
Escalus. Of whence are you?
Duke. Not of this country, though my chance is now
To use it for my time; I am a brother
Of gracious order, late come from the See
In special business from his holiness.

Escalus. What news abroad i' the world? 199

Duke. None, but that there is so great a fever on good-ness, that the dissolution of it must cure it: novelty is only in request; and it is as dangerous to be aged in any kind of course, as it is virtuous to be constant in any undertaking. There is scarce truth enough alive to make societies secure, but security enough to make fellowships accurst. Much upon this riddle runs the wisdom of the world. This news is old enough, yet it is every day's news. I pray you, sir, of what disposition was the duke?

Escalus. One that, above all other strifes, contended es-pecially to know himself. 210

Duke. What pleasure was he given to?

Escalus. Rather rejoicing to see another merry, than merry at any thing which professed to make him rejoice; a gentle-man of all temperance. But leave we him to his events, with a prayer they may prove prosperous, and let me desire to know how you find Claudio prepared. I am made to understand that you have lent him visitation.

Duke. He professes to have received no sinister measure from his judge, but most willingly humbles himself to the determination of justice; yet had he framed to himself, by the instruction of his frailty, many deceiving promises of life, which I by my good leisure have discredited to him, and now is he resolved to die. 223

Escalus. You have paid the heavens your function, and the prisoner the very debt of your calling. I have laboured for the poor gentleman to the extremest shore of my mod-esty; but my brother justice have I found so severe, that he hath forced me to tell him he is indeed justice.

Duke. If his own life answer the straitness of his pro-ceeding, it shall become him well; wherein if he chance to fail, he hath sentenced himself. 231

Escalus. I am going to visit the prisoner. Fare you well.

Duke. Peace be with you!—[*Exeunt Escalus and Provost.*

He who the sword of heaven will bear
Should be as holy as severe;
Pattern in himself to know,
Grace to stand, and virtue go;
More nor less to others paying
Than by self-offences weighing.
Shame to him whose cruel striking   240
Kills for faults of his own liking!
Twice treble shame on Angelo,
To weed my vice and let his grow!
O, what may man within him hide,
Though angel on the outward side!
How may likeness wade in crimes,
Making practice on the times,
To draw with idle spiders' strings
Most ponderous and substantial things!
Craft against vice I must apply: 250
With Angelo to-night shall lie
His old betrothed but despis'd;
So disguise shall, by the disguis'd,
Pay with falsehood false exacting,
And perform an old contracting.   [*Exit.*

INTERIOR OF PRISON (SCENE III.).

ACT IV.

SCENE I.   *The Moated Grange at St. Luke's.*

Enter MARIANA *and a* Boy.

Boy sings.

Take, O, take those lips away,
  That so sweetly were forsworn,
And those eyes, the break of day,
  Lights that do mislead the morn;

But my kisses bring again, bring again.—
Seals of love, but seal'd in vain, seal'd in vain.

Mariana. Break off thy song, and haste thee quick away;
Here comes a man of comfort, whose advice
Hath often still'd my brawling discontent.—   [*Exit Boy.*

Enter DUKE *disguised as before.*

I cry you mercy, sir, and well could wish   10
You had not found me here so musical.
Let me excuse me, and believe me so,
My mirth it much displeas'd, but pleas'd my woe.
    Duke. 'T is good; though music oft hath such a charm
To make bad good, and good provoke to harm.
I pray you, tell me, hath anybody inquired for me here
to-day? much upon this time have I promised here to
meet.
    Mariana. You have not been inquired after; I have sat
here all day.   20

Enter ISABELLA.

    Duke. I do constantly believe you. The time is come
even now. I shall crave your forbearance a little; may be
I will call upon you anon, for some advantage to yourself.
    Mariana. I am always bound to you.   [*Exit.*
    Duke. Very well met, and well come.
What is the news from this good deputy?
    Isabella. He hath a garden circummur'd with brick,
Whose western side is with a vineyard back'd;
And to that vineyard is a planched gate,
That makes his opening with this bigger key: 30
This other doth command a little door
Which from the vineyard to the garden leads;
There have I made my promise
Upon the heavy middle of the night
To call upon him.

Duke. But shall you on your knowledge find this way?

Isabella. I have ta'en a due and wary note upon 't;
With whispering and most guilty diligence,
In action all of precept, he did show me
The way twice o'er.

Duke. Are there no other tokens   40
Between you greed concerning her observance?

Isabella. No, none, but only a repair i' the dark,
And that I have possess'd him my most stay
Can be but brief; for I have made him know
I have a servant comes with me along,
That stays upon me, whose persuasion is
I come about my brother.

Duke. 'T is well borne up.
I have not yet made known to Mariana
A word of this.—What, ho! within! come forth!

Re-enter MARIANA.

I pray you, be acquainted with this maid;   50
She comes to do you good.

Isabella. I do desire the like.

Duke. Do you persuade yourself that I respect you?

Mariana. Good friar, I know you do, and have found it.

Duke. Take, then, this your companion by the hand,
Who hath a story ready for your ear,
I shall attend your leisure: but make haste;
The vaporous night approaches.

Mariana. Will 't please you walk aside?

[*Exeunt Mariana and Isabella.*

Duke. O place and greatness! millions of false eyes
Are stuck upon thee; volumes of report   60
Run with these false and most contrarious quests
Upon thy doings; thousand escapes of wit
Make thee the father of their idle dreams
And rack thee in their fancies.—

Re-enter MARIANA *and* ISABELLA.

                              Welcome, how agreed?
Isabella. She 'll take the enterprise upon her, father,
If you advise it.
Duke.   It is not my consent,
But my entreaty too.
Isabella.   Little have you to say
When you depart from him, but, soft and low,
' Remember now my brother.'
Mariana.   Fear me not.
Duke. Nor, gentle daughter, fear you not at all.   70
He is your husband on a pre-contract;
To bring you thus together, 't is no sin,
Sith that the justice of your title to him
Doth flourish the deceit.   Come, let us go;
Our corn 's to reap, for yet our tilth 's to sow.   [*Exeunt.*

SCENE II.   *A Room in the Prison.*

Enter PROVOST *and* POMPEY.

Provost. Come hither, sirrah.   Can you cut off a man's
head ?
Pompey. If the man be a bachelor, sir, I can; but if he be
a married man, he 's his wife's head, and I can never cut off
a woman's head.
Provost. Come, sir, leave me your snatches, and yield me
a direct answer.   To-morrow morning are to die Claudio and
Barnardine.   Here is in our prison a common executioner,
who in his office lacks a helper: if you will take it on you to
assist him, it shall redeem you from your gyves; if not, you
shall have your full time of imprisonment and your deliverance with an unpitied whipping, for you have been a notorious bawd.   13
Pompey. Sir, I have been an unlawful bawd time out of

mind, but yet I will be content to be a lawful hangman. I would be glad to receive some instruction from my fellow partner.

Provost. What, ho! Abhorson! Where 's Abhorson, there?

Enter ABHORSON.

Abhorson. Do you call, sir?

Provost. Sirrah, here 's a fellow will help you to-morrow in your execution. If you think it meet, compound with him by the year, and let him abide here with you; if not, use him for the present and dismiss him. He cannot plead his estimation with you; he hath been a bawd. 24

Abhorson. A bawd, sir? fie upon him; he will discredit our mystery.

Provost. Go to, sir; you weigh equally; a feather will turn the scale. [*Exit.*

Pompey. Pray, sir, by your good favour,—for surely, sir, a good favour you have, but that you have a hanging look,—do you call, sir, your occupation a mystery? 31

Abhorson. Ay, sir; a mystery.

Pompey. Painting, sir, I have heard say, is a mystery; and your whores, sir, being members of my occupation, using painting, do prove my occupation a mystery; but what mystery there should be in hanging, if I should be hanged, I cannot imagine.

Abhorson. Sir, it is a mystery.

Pompey. Proof?

Abhorson. Every true man's apparel fits your thief. 40

Pompey. If it be too little for your thief, your true man thinks it big enough; if it be too big for your thief, your thief thinks it little enough: so every true man's apparel fits your thief.

Re-enter PROVOST.

Provost. Are you agreed?

Pompey. Sir, I will serve him, for I do find your hangman

is a more penitent trade than your bawd; he doth oftener ask forgiveness.

Provost. You, sirrah, provide your block and your axe to-morrow four o'clock.

Abhorson. Come on, bawd; I will instruct thee in my trade; follow.   51

Pompey. I do desire to learn, sir: and I hope, if you have occasion to use me for your own turn, you shall find me yare; for truly, sir, for your kindness I owe you a good turn.

Provost. Call hither Barnardine and Claudio.—

                            [Exeunt Pompey and Abhorson.

The one has my pity; not a jot the other,
Being a murtherer, though he were my brother.—

                     Enter CLAUDIO.

Look, here 's the warrant, Claudio, for thy death;
'T is now dead midnight, and by eight to-morrow
Thou must be made immortal. Where 's Barnardine?   60

Claudio. As fast lock'd up in sleep as guiltless labour
When it lies starkly in the traveller's bones;
He will not wake.

Provost.   Who can do good on him?
Well, go, prepare yourself. [*Knocking within.*] But, hark, what noise?
Heaven give your spirits comfort!—[*Exit Claudio.*] By and
    by.—
I hope it is some pardon or reprieve
For the most gentle Claudio.

            Enter DUKE *disguised as before.*

                   Welcome, father.

Duke. The best and wholesom'st spirits of the night
Envelop you, good provost! Who call'd here of late?

Provost. None, since the curfew rung.   70

Duke. Not Isabel?

Provost.　　　　No.

Duke.　　　　　They will, then, ere 't be long.

Provost. What comfort is for Claudio?

Duke. There 's some in hope.

Provost.　　　　　　It is a bitter deputy.

Duke. Not so, not so; his life is parallel'd
Even with the stroke and line of his great justice.
He doth with holy abstinence subdue
That in himself which he spurs on his power
To qualify in others. Were he meal'd with that
Which he corrects, then were he tyrannous;
But this being so, he 's just.—[*Knocking within.*] Now are
　　　they come.—　　　　　　　　[*Exit Provost.*
This is a gentle provost; seldom when　　　　　　8।
The steeled gaoler is the friend of men.— [*Knocking within.*
How now! what noise? That spirit 's possess'd with haste
That wounds the unsisting postern with these strokes.

　　　　　Re-enter PROVOST.

Provost. There he must stay until the officer
Arise to let him in; he is call'd up.

Duke. Have you no countermand for Claudio yet,
But he must die to-morrow?

Provost.　　　　None, sir, none.

Duke. As near the dawning, provost, as it is,
You shall hear more ere morning.

Provost.　　　　　　Happily　　　　90
You something know, yet I believe there comes
No countermand; no such example have we.
Besides, upon the very siege of justice
Lord Angelo hath to the public ear
Profess'd the contrary.

　　　　　Enter a Messenger.

　　　　This is his lordship's man.

G

Duke. And here comes Claudio's pardon.

Messenger. [*Giving a paper.*] My lord hath sent you this note ; and by me this further charge, that you swerve not from the smallest article of it, neither in time, matter, or other circumstance. Good morrow; for, as I take it, it is almost day.　　　　　　　　　　　　　　　　　　　　　　　101

　　Provost. I shall obey him.　　　　　　[*Exit Messenger.*

　　Duke. [*Aside*] This is his pardon, purchas'd by such sin

For which the pardoner himself is in.

Hence hath offence his quick celerity,

When it is borne in high authority.

When vice makes mercy, mercy 's so extended,

That for the fault's love is the offender friended.—

Now, sir, what news ?

　　Provost. I told you. Lord Angelo, belike thinking me remiss in mine office, awakens me with this unwonted putting-on; methinks strangely, for he hath not used it before.　　112

　　Duke. Pray you, let 's hear.

　　Provost. [Reads] '*Whatsoever you may hear to* **the contrary,** *let Claudio* **be** *executed by four* **of the clock, and** *in the afternoon Barnardine. For* **my better satisfaction,** *let me have* **Claudio's head sent me by** *five.* **Let this be** *duly performed,* **with a thought that more** *depends* **on it than** *we must yet deliver.* **Thus fail not to do your office, as** *you will answer* **it** *at your peril.'*　　　　　　　　　　　　　　　　　　　120

What say you to this, sir ?

　　Duke. What is that Barnardine who is to be executed in the afternoon ?

　　Provost. A Bohemian born, but here nursed up and bred ; one that is a prisoner nine years old.

　　Duke. How came it that the absent duke had not either delivered him to his liberty or executed him ? I have heard it was ever his manner to do so.

　　Provost. His friends still wrought reprieves for him; and, indeed, his fact, till now in the government of Lord Angelo, came not to an undoubtful proof.   131

Duke. It is now apparent?

Provost. Most manifest, and not denied by himself.

Duke. Hath he borne himself penitently in prison? how seems he to be touched?

Provost. A man that apprehends death no more dreadfully but as a drunken sleep; careless, reckless, and fearless of what 's past, present, or to come; insensible of mortality, and desperately mortal.

Duke. He wants advice.   140

Provost. He will hear none. He hath evermore had the liberty of the prison; give him leave to escape hence, he would not: drunk many times a day, if not many days entirely drunk. We have very oft awaked him, as if to carry him to execution, and showed him a seeming warrant for it; it hath not moved him at all.

Duke. More of him anon. There is written in your brow, provost, honesty and constancy: if I read it not truly, my ancient skill beguiles me; but, in the boldness of my cunning, I will lay myself in hazard. Claudio, whom here you have warrant to execute, is no greater forfeit to the law than Angelo who hath sentenced him. To make you understand this in a manifested effect, I crave but four days' respite; for the which you are to do me both a present and a dangerous courtesy.

Provost. Pray, sir, in what?

Duke. In the delaying death.

Provost. Alack, how may I do it, having the hour limited, and an express command, under penalty, to deliver his head in the view of Angelo? I may make my case as Claudio's, to cross this in the smallest.   161

Duke. By the vow of mine order I warrant you, if my instructions may be your guide. Let this Barnardine be this morning executed, and his head borne to Angelo.

Provost. Angelo hath seen them both, and will discover the favour.

Duke. O, death 's a great disguiser, and you may add to it. Shave the head, and tie the beard, and say it was the desire of the penitent to be so bared before his death; you know the course is common. If any thing fall to you upon this, more than thanks and good fortune, by the saint whom I profess, I will plead against it with my life.   173

Provost. Pardon me, good father; it is against my oath.

Duke. Were you sworn to the duke, or to the deputy?

Provost. To him, and to his substitutes.

Duke. You will think you have made no offence, if the duke avouch the justice of your dealing?

Provost. But what likelihood is in that?

Duke. Not a resemblance, but a certainty. Yet since I see you fearful, that neither my coat, integrity, nor persuasion can with ease attempt you, I will go further than I meant, to pluck all fears out of you. Look you, sir, here is the hand and seal of the duke; you know the character, I doubt not, and the signet is not strange to you.   185

Provost. I know them both.

Duke. The contents of this is the return of the duke; you shall anon over-read it at your pleasure, where you shall find within these two days he will be here. This is a thing that Angelo knows not, for he this very day receives letters of strange tenour: perchance of the duke's death; perchance entering into some monastery; but, by chance, nothing of what is writ. Look, the unfolding star calls up the shepherd. Put not yourself into amazement how these things should be; all difficulties are but easy when they are known. Call your executioner, and off with Barnardine's head; I will give him a present shrift and advise him for a better place. Yet you are amazed; but this shall absolutely resolve you. Come away; it is almost clear dawn.   [*Exeunt.*

SCENE III. *Another Room in the Same.*

Enter POMPEY.

Pompey. I am as well acquainted here as I was in our house of profession; one would think it were Mistress Over-done's own house, for here be many of her old customers. First, here 's young Master Rash; he 's in for a commodity of brown paper and old ginger, nine-score and seventeen pounds, of which he made five marks, ready money: marry, then ginger was not much in request, for the old women were all dead. Then is there here one Master Caper, at the suit of Master Three-pile the mercer, for some four suits of peach-coloured satin, which now peaches him a beggar. Then have we here young Dizy, and young Master Deep-vow, and Mas-ter Copper-spur, and Master Starve-lackey the rapier and dagger man, and young Drop-heir that killed lusty Pudding, and Master Forthright the tilter, and brave Master Shooty the great traveller, and wild Half-can that stabbed Pots, and, I think, forty more, all great doers in our trade, and are now for the Lord's sake.

Enter ABHORSON.

Abhorson. Sirrah, bring Barnardine hither.

Pompey. Master Barnardine! you must rise and be hang-ed, Master Barnardine!   20

Abhorson. What, ho, Barnardine!

Barnardine. [*Within*] A pox o' your throats! Who makes that noise there? What are you?

Pompey. Your friends, sir; the hangman. You must be so good, sir, to rise and be put to death.

Barnardine. [*Within*] Away, you rogue, away! I am sleepy.

Abhorson. Tell him he must awake, and that quickly too.

Pompey. Pray, Master Barnardine, awake till you are ex-ecuted, and sleep afterwards.   30

Abhorson. Go in to him, and fetch him out.

Pompey. He is coming, sir, he is coming; I hear his straw rustle.

Abhorson. Is the axe upon the block, sirrah?

Pompey. Very ready, sir.

Enter BARNARDINE.

Barnardine. How now, Abhorson? what 's the news with you?

Abhorson. Truly, sir, I would desire you to clap into your prayers; for, look you, the warrant 's come.

Barnardine. You rogue, I have been drinking all night; I am not fitted for 't.   41

Pompey. O, the better, sir; for he that drinks all night, and is hanged betimes in the morning, may sleep the sounder all the next day.

Abhorson. Look you, sir; here comes your ghostly father: do we jest now, think you?

Enter DUKE *disguised as before.*

Duke. Sir, induced by my charity, and hearing how hastily you are to depart, I am come to advise you, comfort you, and pray with you.

Barnardine. Friar, not I; I have been drinking hard all night, and I will have more time to prepare me, or they shall beat out my brains with billets. I will not consent to die this day, that 's certain.   53

Duke. O, sir, you must; and therefore I beseech you
Look forward on the journey you shall go.

Barnardine. I swear I will not die to-day for any man's persuasion.

Duke. But hear you,—

Barnardine. Not a word; if you have any thing to say to me, come to my ward, for thence will not I to-day.   [*Exit.*

Duke. Unfit to live or die. O gravel heart! 61
After him, fellows; bring him to the block.
  [*Exeunt Abhorson and Pompey.*

Re-enter PROVOST.

Provost. Now, sir, how do you find the prisoner?
Duke. A creature unprepar'd, unmeet for death;
And to transport him in the mind he is
Were damnable.
Provost.   Here in the prison, father,
There died this morning of a cruel fever
One Ragozine, a most notorious pirate,
A man of Claudio's years; his beard and head
Just of his colour. What if we do omit 70
This reprobate till he were well inclin'd
And satisfy the deputy with the visage
Of Ragozine, more like to Claudio?
Duke. O, 't is an accident that heaven provides!
Dispatch it presently; the hour draws on
Prefix'd by Angelo: see this be done,
And sent according to command, whiles I
Persuade this rude wretch willingly to die.
Provost. This shall be done, good father, presently.
But Barnardine must die this afternoon; 80
And how shall we continue Claudio,
To save me from the danger that might come
If he were known alive?
Duke.   Let this be done:
Put them in secret holds, both Barnardine and Claudio.
Ere twice the sun hath made his journal greeting
To the under generation, you shall find
Your safety manifested.
Provost. I am your free dependant.
Duke. Quick, dispatch, and send the head to Angelo.—
  [*Exit Provost.*

Now will I write letters to Angelo,—   90
The provost, he shall bear them,—whose contents
Shall witness to him I am near at home,
And that, by great injunctions, I am bound
To enter publicly.   Him I 'll desire
To meet me at the consecrated fount
A league below the city; and from thence,
By cold gradation and well-balanc'd form,
We shall proceed with Angelo.

Re-enter PROVOST.

Provost. Here is the head ; I 'll carry it myself.
Duke. Convenient is it.   Make a swift return,   100
For I would commune with you of such things
That want no ear but yours.
Provost.   I 'll make all speed. | *Exit.*
Isabella. [*Within*]· Peace, ho, be here !
Duke. The tongue of Isabel.   She 's come to know
If yet her brother's pardon be come hither ;
But I will keep her ignorant of her good,
To make her heavenly comforts of despair,
When it is least expected.

Enter ISABELLA.

Isabella.   Ho, by your leave !
Duke. Good morning to you, fair and gracious daughter.
Isabella. The better, given me by so holy a man.   110
Hath yet the deputy sent my brother's pardon ?
Duke. He hath releas'd him, Isabel, from the world ;
His head is off and sent to Angelo.
Isabella. Nay, but it is not so.
Duke. It is no other ; show your wisdom, daughter,
In your close patience.
Isabella. O, I will to him and pluck out his eyes !
Duke. You shall not be admitted to his sight.

Isabella. Unhappy Claudio! wretched Isabel!
Injurious world! most damned Angelo! 120
Duke. This nor hurts him nor profits you a jot.
Forbear it therefore; give your cause to heaven.
Mark what I say, which you shall find
By every syllable a faithful verity:
The duke comes home to-morrow;—nay, dry your eyes;
One of our covent, and his confessor,
Gives me this instance. Already he hath carried
Notice to Escalus and Angelo,
Who do prepare to meet him at the gates,
There to give up their power. If you can pace your wisdom
In that good path that I would wish it, go; 131
And you shall have your bosom on this wretch,
Grace of the duke, revenges to your heart,
And general honour.
Isabella.   I am directed by you.
Duke. This letter, then, to Friar Peter give;
'T is that he sent me of the duke's return.
Say, by this token, I desire his company
At Mariana's house to-night. Her cause and yours
I 'll perfect him withal, and he shall bring you
Before the duke, and to the head of Angelo 140
Accuse him home and home. For my poor self,
I am combined by a sacred vow
And shall be absent. Wend you with this letter.
Command these fretting waters from your eyes
With a light heart; trust not my holy order,
If I pervert your course.—Who 's here?

Enter LUCIO.

Lucio. Good even. Friar, where 's the provost?
Duke. Not within, sir.
Lucio. O pretty Isabella, I am pale at mine heart to see
thine eyes so red; thou must be patient. I am fain to dine

and sup with water and bran; I dare not for my head fill my belly; one fruitful meal would set me to 't.   But they say the duke will be here to-morrow.   By my troth, Isabel, I loved thy brother; if the old fantastical duke of dark corners had been at home, he had lived.   [*Exit Isabella.*

Duke. Sir, the duke is marvellous little beholding to your reports; but the best is, he lives not in them.

Lucio. Friar, thou knowest not the duke so well as I do; he 's a better woodman than thou takest him for.   159

Duke. Well, you 'll answer this one day.   Fare ye well.

Lucio. Nay, tarry; I 'll go along with thee.   I can tell thee pretty tales of the duke.

Duke. You have told me too many of him already, sir, if they be true; if not true, none were enough.

Lucio. I was once before him for getting a wench with child.

Duke. Did you such a thing?

Lucio. Yes, marry, did I; but I was fain to forswear it: they would else have married me to the rotten medlar.

Duke. Sir, your company is fairer than honest.   Rest you well.   171

Lucio. By my troth, I 'll go with thee to the lane's end. If bawdy talk offend you, we 'll have very little of it.   Nay, friar, I am a kind of burr; I shall stick.   [*Exeunt.*

SCENE IV.   *A Room in Angelo's House.*

Enter ANGELO *and* ESCALUS.

Escalus. Every letter he hath writ hath disvouched other.

Angelo. In most uneven and distracted manner.   His actions show much like to madness; pray heaven his wisdom be not tainted!   And why meet him at the gates, and redeliver our authorities there?

Escalus. I guess not.

Angelo. And why should we proclaim it in an hour before

his entering, that if any crave redress of injustice, they should
exhibit their petitions in the street?   9

Escalus. He shows his reason for that: to have a dispatch
of complaints, and to deliver us from devices hereafter, which
shall then have no power to stand against us.

Angelo. Well, I beseech you, let it be proclaimed betimes
i' the morn; I 'll call you at your house.   Give notice to
such men of sort and suit as are to meet him.

Escalus. I shall, sir.   Fare you well.

Angelo. Good night.—   [*Exit Escalus.*
This deed unshapes me quite, makes me unpregnant
And dull to all proceedings.   A deflower'd maid!
And by an eminent body that enforc'd   20
The law against it!   But that her tender shame
Will not proclaim against her maiden loss,
How might she tongue me!   Yet reason dares her no;
For my authority bears so credent bulk,
That no particular scandal once can touch
But it confounds the breather.   He should have liv'd,
Save that his riotous youth, with dangerous sense,
Might in the times to come have ta'en revenge,
By so receiving a dishonour'd life
With ransom of such shame.   Would yet he had liv'd!   30
Alack, when once our grace we have forgot,
Nothing goes right; we would, and we would not.   [*Exit.*

SCENE V.   *Fields without the Town.*

Enter DUKE *in his own habit, and* FRIAR PETER.

Duke. These letters at fit time deliver me. [*Giving letters.*
The provost knows our purpose and our plot.
The matter being afoot, keep your instruction,
And hold you ever to our special drift,
Though sometimes you do blench from this to that,
As cause doth minister.   Go call at Flavius' house,

And tell him where I stay: give the like notice
To Valentinus, Rowland, and to Crassus,
And bid them bring the trumpets to the gate;
But send me Flavius first.
 Friar Peter.   It shall be speeded well. [*Exit.*

Enter VARRIUS.

Duke. I thank thee, Varrius; thou hast made good haste.
Come, we will walk. There 's other of our friends 12
Will greet us here anon, my gentle Varrius. [*Exeunt.*

SCENE VI. *Street near the* City Gate.
Enter ISABELLA *and* MARIANA.

Isabella. To speak so indirectly I am loath.
I would say the truth; but to accuse him so,
That is your part : yet I am advis'd to do it,
He says, to veil full purpose.
 Mariana.   Be rul'd by him.
 Isabella. Besides, he tells me that, if peradventure
He speak against me on the adverse side,
I should not think it strange; for 't is a physic
That 's bitter to sweet end.
 Mariana. I would Friar Peter—
 Isabella.   O, peace! the friar is come.

Enter FRIAR PETER.

Friar Peter. Come, I have found you out a stand most fit,
Where you may have such vantage on the duke, 11
He shall not pass you. Twice have the trumpets sounded;
The generous and gravest citizens
Have hent the gates, and very near upon
The duke is entering : therefore, hence, away! [*Exeunt.*

ACT V.

SCENE I. *The City Gate.*

MARIANA *veiled*, ISABELLA, *and* FRIAR PETER, *at their stand.*
Enter DUKE, VARRIUS, Lords, ANGELO, ESCALUS, LUCIO,
PROVOST, Officers, *and* Citizens, *at several doors.*

Duke. My very worthy cousin, fairly met !—
Our old and faithful friend, we are glad to see you.

Angelo.
Escalus. } Happy return be to your royal grace !

Duke. Many and hearty thankings to you both.
We have made inquiry of you; and we hear
Such goodness of your justice, that our soul
Cannot but yield you forth to public thanks,
Forerunning more requital.

    Angelo.   You make my bonds still greater.

    Duke. O, your desert speaks loud; and I should wrong
      it,
To lock it in the wards of covert bosom,   10
When it deserves, with characters of brass,
A forted residence 'gainst the tooth of time
And razure of oblivion. Give me your hand,
And let the subject see, to make them know
That outward courtesies would fain proclaim
Favours that keep within.—Come, Escalus,
You must walk by us on our other hand;
And good supporters are you.

    FRIAR PETER *and* ISABELLA *come forward.*

    Friar Peter. Now is your time; speak loud and kneel be-
      fore him.

    Isabella. Justice, O royal duke! Vail your regard   20
Upon a wrong'd, I would fain have said, a maid !
O worthy prince, dishonour not your eye
By throwing it on any other object
Till you have heard me in my true complaint
And given me justice, justice, justice, justice !

    Duke. Relate your wrongs; in what? by whom? be brief.
Here is Lord Angelo shall give you justice ;
Reveal yourself to him.

    Isabella.   O worthy duke,
You bid me seek redemption of the devil.
Hear me yourself; for that which I must speak   30

Must either punish me, not being believ'd,
Or wring redress from you.   Hear me, O hear me, here !
   Angelo. My lord, her wits, I fear me, are not firm ;
She hath been a suitor to me for her brother
Cut off by course of justice,—
   Isabella.   By course of justice !
   Angelo. And she will speak most bitterly and strange.
   Isabella. Most strange, but yet most truly, will I speak :
That Angelo 's forsworn ; is it not strange ?
That Angelo 's a murtherer ; is 't not strange ?
That Angelo is an adulterous thief,   40
An hypocrite, a virgin-violator ;
Is it not strange and strange ?
   Duke.   Nay, it is ten times strange.
   Isabella. It is not truer he is Angelo
Than this is all as true as it is strange.
Nay, it is ten times true ; for truth is truth
To the end of reckoning.
   Duke.   Away with her !—Poor soul,
She speaks this in the infirmity of sense.
   Isabella. O prince, I conjure thee, as thou believ'st
There is another comfort than this world,
That thou neglect me not, with that opinion   50
That I am touch'd with madness !   Make not impossible
That which but seems unlike : 't is not impossible
But one, the wicked'st caitiff on the ground,
May seem as shy, as grave, as just, as absolute
As Angelo ; even so may Angelo,
In all his dressings, characts, titles, forms,
Be an arch-villain ; believe it, royal prince.
If he be less, he 's nothing ; but he 's more,
Had I more name for badness.
   Duke.   By mine honesty,
If she be mad,—as I believe no other,—   60
Her madness hath the oddest frame of sense,

Such a dependency of thing on thing,
As e'er I heard in madness.
 Isabella.   O gracious duke,
Harp not on that, nor do not banish reason
For inequality; but let your reason serve
To make the truth appear where it seems hid,
And hide the false seems true.
 Duke.   Many that are not mad
Have, sure, more lack of reason.—What would you say?
 Isabella. I am the sister of one Claudio,
Condemn'd upon the act of fornication   70
To lose his head, condemn'd by Angelo.
I, in probation of a sisterhood,
Was sent to by my brother; one Lucio
As then the messenger,—
 Lucio.   That 's I, an 't like your grace.
I came to her from Claudio, and desir'd her
To try her gracious fortune with Lord Angelo
For her poor brother's pardon.
 Isabella.   That 's he indeed.
 Duke. You were not bid to speak.
 Lucio.   No, my good lord;
Nor wish'd to hold my peace.
 Duke.   I wish you now, then:
Pray you, take note of it; and when you have   80
A business for yourself, pray heaven you then
Be perfect.
 Lucio. I warrant your honour.
 Duke. The warrant 's for yourself; take heed to 't.
 Isabella. This gentleman told somewhat of my tale,—
 Lucio. Right.
 Duke. It may be right, but you are i' the wrong
To speak before your time.—Proceed.
 Isabella.   I went
To this pernicious caitiff deputy,—

Duke. That 's somewhat madly spoken.

Isabella.   Pardon it;

The phrase is to the matter.   90

Duke. Mended again.   The matter; proceed.

Isabella. In brief, to set the needless process by,

How I persuaded, how I pray'd, and kneel'd,

How he refell'd me, and how I replied,—

For this was of much length,—the vile conclusion

I now begin with grief and shame to utter.

He would not, but by gift of my chaste body

To his concupiscible intemperate lust,

Release my brother; and, after much debatement,

My sisterly remorse confutes mine honour,   100

And I did yield to him; but the next morn betimes,

His purpose surfeiting, he sends a warrant

For my poor brother's head.

Duke.   This is most likely!

Isabella. O, that it were as like as it is true!

Duke. By heaven, fond wretch, thou know'st not what thou

          speak'st,

Or else thou art suborn'd against his honour

In hateful practice.   First, his integrity

Stands without blemish.   Next, it imports no reason

That with such vehemency he should pursue

Faults proper to himself.   If he had so offended,   110

He would have weigh'd thy brother by himself,

And not have cut him off.   Some one hath set you on;

Confess the truth, and say by whose advice

Thou cam'st here to complain.

Isabella.   And is this all?

Then, O you blessed ministers above,.

Keep me in patience, and with ripen'd time

Unfold the evil which is here wrapt up

In countenance!—Heaven shield your grace from woe,

As I, thus wrong'd, hence unbelieved go!

H

Duke. I know you 'd fain be gone.—An officer!—   120
To prison with her!—Shall we thus permit
A blasting and a scandalous breath to fall
On him so near us? This needs must be a practice.
Who knew of your intent and coming hither?
    Isabella. One that I would were here, Friar Lodowick?
    Duke. A ghostly father, belike.—Who knows that Lodo-
        wick?
    Lucio. My lord, I know him; 't is a meddling friar.
I do not like the man; had he been lay, my lord,
For certain words he spake against your grace
In your retirement, I had swing'd him soundly.   130
    Duke. Words against me! this' a good friar, belike!
And to set on this wretched woman here
Against our substitute!—Let this friar be found.
    Lucio. But yesternight, my lord, she and that friar,
I saw them at the prison,—a saucy friar,
A very scurvy fellow.
    Friar Peter. Blessed be your royal grace!
I have stood by, my lord, and I have heard
Your royal ear abus'd. First, hath this woman
Most wrongfully accus'd your substitute,   140
Who is as free from touch or soil with her
As she from one ungot.
    Duke.   We did believe no less.
Know you that Friar Lodowick that she speaks of?
    Friar Peter. I know him for a man divine and holy;
Not scurvy, nor a temporary meddler,
As he 's reported by this gentleman,
And, on my trust, a man that never yet
Did, as he vouches, misreport your grace.
    Lucio. My lord, most villanously; believe it.
    Friar Peter. Well, he in time may come to clear himself,
But at this instant he is sick, my lord,   151
Of a strange fever. Upon his mere request,

Being come to knowledge that there was complaint
Intended 'gainst Lord Angelo, came I hither,
To speak, as from his mouth, what he doth know
Is true and false, and what he with his oath
And all probation will make up full clear,
Whensoever he 's convented. First, for this woman,
To justify this worthy nobleman,
So vulgarly and personally accus'd,   160
Her shall you hear disproved to her eyes,
Till she herself confess it.
  Duke.   Good friar, let 's hear it.—
    [*Isabella is carried off guarded; and Mariana*
     comes forward.
Do you not smile at this, Lord Angelo?
O heaven, the vanity of wretched fools!—
Give us some seats.—Come, cousin Angelo;
In this I 'll be impartial; be you judge
Of your own cause.—Is this the witness, friar?
First, let her show her face, and after speak.
  Mariana. Pardon, my lord; I will not show my face
Until my husband bid me.   170
  Duke. What, are you married?
  Mariana. No, my lord.
  Duke. Are you a maid?
  Mariana. No, my lord.
  Duke. A widow, then?
  Mariana. Neither, my lord.
  Duke. Why, you are nothing then; neither maid, widow,
nor wife?
  Lucio. My lord, she may be a punk; for many of them are
neither maid, widow, nor wife.   180
  Duke. Silence that fellow; I would he had some cause
To prattle for himself.
  Lucio. Well, my lord.
  Mariana. My lord, I do confess I ne'er was married;

And I confess besides I am no maid :
I have known my husband ; yet my husband
Knows not that ever he knew me.
   Lucio. He was drunk then, my lord ; it can be no better.
   Duke. For the benefit of silence, would thou wert so too!
   Lucio. Well, my lord.   190
   Duke. This is no witness for Lord Angelo.
   Mariana. Now I come to 't, my lord :
She that accuses him of fornication,
In self-same manner doth accuse my husband,
And charges him, my lord, with such a time
When I 'll depose I had him in mine arms
With all the effect of love.
   Angelo. Charges she more than me?
   Mariana.   Not that I know.
   Duke. No? you say your husband.
   Mariana. Why, just, my lord, and that is Angelo,   200
Who thinks he knows that he ne'er knew my body,
But knows, he thinks, that he knows Isabel's.
   Angelo. This is a strange abuse.—Let 's see thy face.
   Mariana. My husband bids me ; now I will unmask.—
                                  [Unveiling.

This is that face, thou cruel Angelo,
Which once thou swor'st was worth the looking on ;
This is the hand which, with a vow'd contract,
Was fast belock'd in thine ; this is the body
That took away the match from Isabel,
And did supply thee at thy garden-house   210
In her imagin'd person.
   Duke.   Know you this woman?
   Lucio. Carnally, she says.
   Duke.   Sirrah, no more !
   Lucio. Enough, my lord.
   Angelo. My lord, I must confess I know this woman ;
And five years since there was some speech of marriage

Betwixt myself and her, which was broke off,
Partly for that her promised proportions
Came short of composition, but in chief
For that her reputation was disvalued
In levity: since which time of five years   220
I never spake with her, saw her, nor heard from her,
Upon my faith and honour.
 Mariana.   Noble prince,
As there comes light from heaven and words from breath,
As there is sense in truth and truth in virtue,
I am affianc'd this man's wife as strongly
As words could make up vows; and, my good lord,
But Tuesday night last gone in 's garden-house
He knew me as a wife. As this is true,
Let me in safety raise me from my knees;
Or else for ever be confixed here,   230
A marble monument!
 Angelo.   I did but smile till now:
Now, good my lord, give me the scope of justice;
My patience here is touch'd. I do perceive
These poor informal women are no more
But instruments of some more mightier member
That sets them on. Let me have way, my lord,
To find this practice out.
 Duke.   Ay, with my heart;
And punish them to your height of pleasure.—
Thou foolish friar, and thou pernicious woman,
Compact with her that 's gone, think'st thou thy oaths,   240
Though they would swear down each particular saint,
Were testimonies against his worth and credit
That 's seal'd in approbation? —You, Lord Escalus,
Sit with my cousin ; lend him your kind pains
To find out this abuse, whence 't is deriv'd.—
There is another friar that set them on;
Let him be sent for.

Friar Peter. Would he were here, my lord! for he indeed
Hath set the women on to this complaint.
Your provost knows the place where he abides,   250
And he may fetch him.
      Duke.   Go do it instantly.— [*Exit Provost.*
And you, my noble and well-warranted cousin,
Whom it concerns to hear this matter forth,
Do with your injuries as seems you best,
In any chastisement. I for a while will leave you;
But stir not you till you have well determin'd
Upon these slanderers.
      Escalus. My lord, we 'll do it throughly.—   [*Exit Duke.*
Signior Lucio, did not you say you knew that Friar Lodowick
to be a dishonest person?   260
      Lucio. Cucullus non facit monachum : honest in nothing
but in his clothes; and one that hath spoke most villainous
speeches of the duke.
      Escalus. We shall entreat you to abide here till he come,
and enforce them against him; we shall find this friar a
notable fellow.
      Lucio. As any in Vienna, on my word.
      Escalus. Call that same Isabel here once again ; I would
speak with her.—[*Exit an Attendant.*] Pray you, my lord,
give me leave to question; you shall see how I 'll handle
her.   271
      Lucio. Not better than he, by her own report.
      Escalus. Say you?
      Lucio. Marry, sir, I think, if you handled her privately,
she would sooner confess; perchance, publicly, she 'll be
ashamed.
      Escalus. I will go darkly to work with her.
      Lucio. That 's the way ; for women are light at midnight.

Re-enter Officers *with* ISABELLA; *and* PROVOST *with the* DUKE *in his friar's habit.*

Escalus. Come on, mistress. — Here 's a gentlewoman denies all that you have said.   280

Lucio. My lord, here comes the rascal I spoke of; here with the provost.

Escalus. In very good time; speak not you to him till we call upon you.

Lucio. Mum.

Escalus. Come, sir; did you set these women on to slander Lord Angelo? they have confessed you did.

Duke. 'T is false.

Escalus. How! know you where you are?

Duke. Respect to your great place! and let the devil   290
Be sometime honour'd for his burning throne!—
Where is the duke? 't is he should hear me speak.

Escalus. The duke 's in us, and we will hear you speak;
Look you speak justly.

Duke. Boldly, at least.—But, O, poor souls,
Come you to seek the lamb here of the fox?
Good night to your redress! Is the duke gone?
Then is your cause gone too. The duke 's unjust,
Thus to retort your manifest appeal,
And put your trial in the villain's mouth   300
Which here you come to accuse.

Lucio. This is the rascal; this is he I spoke of.

Escalus. Why, thou unreverend and unhallow'd friar,
Is 't not enough thou hast suborn'd these women
To accuse this worthy man, but, in foul mouth
And in the witness of his proper ear,
To call him villain? and then to glance from him
To the duke himself, to tax him with injustice?—
Take him hence; to the rack with him!—We 'll touze you
Joint by joint, but we will know his purpose.   310
What, unjust!

Duke.   Be not so hot; the duke
Dare no more stretch this finger of mine than he
Dare rack his own; his subject am I not,
Nor here provincial. My business in this state
Made me a looker-on here in Vienna,
Where I have seen corruption boil and bubble
Till it o'er-run the stew; laws for all faults,
But faults so countenanc'd, that the strong statutes
Stand like the forfeits in a barber's shop,
As much in mock as mark.   320
     Escalus. Slander to the state! Away with him to
          prison!
     Angelo. What can you vouch against him, Signior Lu-
          cio?
Is this the man that you did tell us of?
     Lucio. 'T is he, my lord. — Come hither, goodman bald-
pate; do you know me?
     Duke. I remember you, sir, by the sound of your voice; I
met you at the prison, in the absence of the duke.
     Lucio. O, did you so? And do you remember what you
said of the duke?
     Duke. Most notedly, sir.   330
     Lucio. Do you so, sir? And was the duke a fleshmonger,
a fool, and a coward, as you then reported him to be?
     Duke. You must, sir, change persons with me, ere you
make that my report; you, indeed, spoke so of him, and
much more, much worse.
     Lucio. O thou damnable fellow! Did not I pluck thee
by the nose for thy speeches?
     Duke. I protest I love the duke as I love myself.
     Angelo. Hark, how the villain would close now, after his
treasonable abuses!   340
     Escalus. Such a fellow is not to be talked withal. — Away
with him to prison! — Where is the provost? — Away with him
to prison! lay bolts enough upon him; let him speak no

more.—Away with those giglots too, and with the other con-
federate companion!

Duke. [*To Provost*] Stay, sir; stay awhile.

Angelo. What, resists he?—Help him, Lucio.

Lucio. Come, sir; come, sir; come, sir; foh, sir! Why,
you bald-pated, lying rascal, you must be hooded, must you?
Show your knave's visage, with a pox to you! show your
sheep-biting face, and be hanged an hour! Will 't not off?

[*Pulls off the Friar's hood and discovers the Duke.*

Duke. Thou art the first knave that e'er mad'st a
duke.—

First, provost, let me bail these gentle three.— 353

[*To Lucio*] Sneak not away, sir, for the friar and you
Must have a word anon.—Lay hold on him.

Lucio. This may prove worse than hanging.

Duke. [*To Escalus*] What you have spoke I pardon; sit
you down.

We 'll borrow place of him.—[*To Angelo*] Sir, by your leave.
Hast thou or word, or wit, or impudence,
That yet can do thee office? If thou hast, 360
Rely upon it till my tale be heard,
And hold no longer out.

Angelo.   O my dread lord,
I should be guiltier than my guiltiness,
To think I can be undiscernible,
When I perceive your grace, like power divine,
Hath look'd upon my passes. Then, good prince,
No longer session hold upon my shame,
But let my trial be mine own confession.
Immediate sentence then and sequent death
Is all the grace I beg.

Duke.   Come hither, Mariana 370
Say, wast thou e'er contracted to this woman?

Angelo. I was, my lord.

Duke. Go take her hence, and marry her instantly.—

Do you the office, friar; which consummate,
Return him here again.—Go with him, provost.
            [*Exeunt Angelo, Mariana, Friar Peter, and Provost.*
Escalus. My lord, I am more amaz'd at his dishonour
Than at the strangeness of it.
    Duke.   Come hither, Isabel.
Your friar is now your prince : as I was then
Advertising and holy to your business,
Not changing heart with habit, I am still   380
Attorney'd at your service.
    Isabella.   O, give me pardon,
That I, your vassal, have employ'd and pain'd
Your unknown sovereignty!
    Duke.   You are pardon'd, Isabel ;
And now, dear maid, be you as free to us.
Your brother's death, I know, sits at your heart ;
And you may marvel why I obscur'd myself,
Labouring to save his life, and would not rather
Make rash remonstrance of my hidden power
Than let him so be lost.   O most kind maid,
It was the swift celerity of his death,   390
Which I did think with slower foot came on,
That brain'd my purpose.   But, peace be with him !
That life is better life, past fearing death,
Than that which lives to fear.   Make it your comfort,
So happy is your brother.
    Isabella.   I do, my lord.

Re-enter ANGELO, MARIANA, FRIAR PETER, *and* PROVOST.

Duke. For this new-married man approaching here,
Whose salt imagination yet hath wrong'd
Your well defended honour, you must pardon
For Mariana's sake ; but as he adjudg'd your brother,—
Being criminal, in double violation   400
Of sacred chastity and of promise-breach

Thereon dependent, for your brother's life,—
The very mercy of the law cries out
Most audible, even from his proper tongue,
'An Angelo for Claudio, death for death!'
Haste still pays haste, and leisure answers leisure;
Like doth quit like, and MEASURE still FOR MEASURE.—
Then, Angelo, thy fault 's thus manifested,
Which, though thou wouldst deny, denies thee vantage.
We do condemn thee to the very block   410
Where Claudio stoop'd to death, and with like haste.—
Away with him!
    Mariana.   O my most gracious lord,
I hope you will not mock me with a husband.
    Duke. It is your husband mock'd you with a husband.
Consenting to the safeguard of your honour,
I thought your marriage fit; else imputation,
For that he knew you, might reproach your life
And choke your good to come. For his possessions,
Although by confiscation they are ours,
We do instate and widow you withal,   420
To buy you a better husband.
    Mariana.   O my dear lord,
I crave no other, nor no better man.
    Duke. Never crave him; we are definitive.
    Mariana. Gentle my liege,—   [*Kneeling.*
    Duke.   You do but lose your labour.—
Away with him to death!—[*To Lucio*] Now, sir, to you.
    Mariana. O my good lord!—Sweet Isabel, take my part;
Lend me your knees, and all my life to come
I 'll lend you all my life to do you service.
    Duke. Against all sense you do importune her.
Should she kneel down in mercy of this fact,   430
Her brother's ghost his paved bed would break,
And take her hence in horror.
    Mariana.   Isabel,

Sweet Isabel, do yet but kneel by me;
Hold up your hands, say nothing; I 'll speak all.
They say, best men are moulded out of faults,
And, for the most, become much more the better
For being a little bad; so may my husband.
O Isabel, will you not lend a knee?
    Duke. He dies for Claudio's death.
    Isabella.   Most bounteous sir, [*Kneeling.*
Look, if it please you, on this man condemn'd,   410
As if my brother liv'd.   I partly think
A due sincerity govern'd his deeds,
Till he did look on me; since it is so,
Let him not die.   My brother had but justice,
In that he did the thing for which he died.
For Angelo,
His act did not o'ertake his bad intent,
And must be buried but as an intent
That perish'd by the way.   Thoughts are no subjects—
Intents but merely thoughts.
    Mariana.   Merely, my lord.   450
    Duke. Your suit 's unprofitable; stand up, I say.—
I have bethought me of another fault.—
Provost, how came it Claudio was beheaded
At an unusual hour?
    Provost.   It was commanded so.
    Duke. Had you a special warrant for the deed?
    Provost. No, my good lord; it was by private message.
    Duke. For which I do discharge you of your office;
Give up your keys.
    Provost.   Pardon me, noble lord.
I thought it was a fault, but knew it not,
Yet did repent me, after more advice;   460
For testimony whereof, one in the prison,
That should by private order else have died,
I have reserv'd alive.

Duke.   What 's he?

Provost.   His name is Barnardine.

Duke. I would thou hadst done so by Claudio.—
Go fetch him hither; let me look upon him. [*Exit Provost.*

Escalus. I am sorry, one so learned and so wise
As you, Lord Angelo, have still appear'd,
Should slip so grossly, both in the heat of blood,
And lack of temper'd judgment afterward.

Angelo. I am sorry that such sorrow I procure,   470
And so deep sticks it in my penitent heart
That I crave death more willingly than mercy;
'T is my deserving, and I do entreat it.

Re-enter PROVOST, *with* BARNARDINE, CLAUDIO *muffled, and*
JULIET.

Duke. Which is that Barnardine?

Provost.   This, my lord.

Duke. There was a friar told me of this man.—
Sirrah, thou art said to have a stubborn soul,
That apprehends no further than this world,
And squar'st thy life according. Thou 'rt condemn'd;
But, for those earthly faults, I quit them all,
And pray thee take this mercy to provide   480
For better times to come.—Friar, advise him;
I leave him to your hand.—What muffled fellow 's that?

Provost. This is another prisoner that I sav'd,
Who should have died when Claudio lost his head,
As like almost to Claudio as himself.   [*Unmuffles Claudio.*

Duke. [*To Isabella*] If he be like your brother, for his sake
Is he pardon'd; and, for your lovely sake,
Give me your hand, and say you will be mine,
He is my brother too;—but fitter time for that.
By this Lord Angelo perceives he 's safe;   490
Methinks I see a quickening in his eye.—
Well, Angelo, your evil quits you well:

Look that you love your wife; her worth worth yours.—
I find an apt remission in myself;
And yet here 's one in place I cannot pardon.—
[*To Lucio*] You, sirrah, that knew me for a fool, a coward,
One all of luxury, an ass, a madman,
Wherein have I deserved so of you,
That you extol me thus?

    Lucio. Faith, my lord, I spoke it but according to the trick.
If you will hang me for it, you may; but I had rather it
would please you I might be whipt.   502

    Duke. Whipt first, sir, and hang'd after.—
Proclaim it, provost, round about the city,
If any woman 's wrong'd by this lewd fellow—
As I have heard him swear himself there 's one
Whom he begot with child—let her appear,
And he shall marry her; the nuptial finish'd,
Let him be whipt and hang'd.

    Lucio. I beseech your highness, do not marry me to a
whore. Your highness said even now, I made you a duke;
good my lord, do not recompense me in making me a cuckold.

    Duke. Upon mine honour, thou shalt marry her.   513
Thy slanders I forgive, and therewithal
Remit thy other forfeits.—Take him to prison,
And see our pleasure herein executed.

    Lucio. Marrying a punk, my lord, is pressing to death,
whipping, and hanging.

    Duke. Slandering a prince deserves it.—

                    [*Exeunt Officers with Lucio.*
She, Claudio, that you wrong'd, look you restore.—   520
Joy to you, Mariana!—Love her, Angelo;
I have confess'd her and I know her virtue.—
Thanks, good friend Escalus, for thy much goodness;
There 's more behind that is more gratulate.—
Thanks, provost, for thy care and secrecy;
We shall employ thee in a worthier place.—

Forgive him, Angelo, that brought you home
The head of Ragozine for Claudio's ;
The offence pardons itself.—Dear Isabel,
I have a motion much imports your good,   530
Whereto if you 'll a willing ear incline,
What 's mine is yours and what is yours is mine.—
So, bring us to our palace, where we 'll show
What 's yet behind, that 's meet you all should know. [*Exeunt.*

THE NUNNERY.

Gentle Isabella,
Turn you the key, and know his business of him (i. 5. 7).

Here is the hand and seal of the duke (iv. 2. 183).

NOTES.

ABBREVIATIONS USED IN THE NOTES.

Abbott (or Gr.), Abbott's *Shakespearian Grammar* (third edition).
A. S., Anglo-Saxon.
A. V., Authorized Version of the Bible (1611).
B. and F., Beaumont and Fletcher.
B. J., Ben Jonson.
Camb. ed., "Cambridge edition" of Shakespeare, edited by Clark and Wright.
Cf. (*confer*), compare.
Clarke, "Cassell's Illustrated Shakespeare," edited by Charles and Mary Cowden-Clarke (London, n. d.).
Coll., Collier (second edition).
Coll. MS., Manuscript Corrections of Second Folio, edited by Collier.
D., Dyce (second edition).
H., Hudson ("Harvard" edition).
Halliwell, J. O. Halliwell (folio ed. of Shakespeare).
Id. (*idem*), the same.
J. H., J. Hunter's ed. of *M. for M.* (London, 1873).
K., Knight (second edition).
Nares, *Glossary*, edited by Halliwell and Wright (London, 1859).
Prol., Prologue.
S., Shakespeare.
Schmidt, A. Schmidt's *Shakespeare-Lexicon* (Berlin, 1874).
Sr., Singer.
St., Staunton.
Theo., Theobald.
V., Verplanck.
W., R. Grant White.
Walker, Wm. Sidney Walker's *Critical Examination of the Text of Shakespeare* (London, 1860).
Warb., Warburton.
Wb., Webster's Dictionary (revised quarto edition of 1879).
Worc., Worcester's Dictionary (quarto edition).

The abbreviations of the names of Shakespeare's Plays will be readily understood ; as *T. N.* for *Twelfth Night, Cor.* for *Coriolanus,* 3 *Hen. VI.* for *The Third Part of King Henry the Sixth,* etc. *P. P.* refers to *The Passionate Pilgrim* ; *V.* and *A.* to *Venus and Adonis* ; *L. C.* to *Lover's Complaint* ; and *Sonn.* to the *Sonnets.*

When the abbreviation of the name of a play is followed by a reference to *page,* Rolfe's edition of the play is meant.

The numbers of the lines (except for the present play) are those of the "Globe" ed. or of the American reprint of that ed.

NOTES.

Look, the unfolding star calls up the shepherd (iv. 2. 192).

INTRODUCTION.

WHETSTONE'S " PROMOS AND CASSANDRA."—How little Shakespeare
was really indebted to this earlier play (see p. 12 above) may be inferred
from the following specimen of it (quoted by Knight), which may be com-
pared with the corresponding scene (ii. 2) of *Measure for Measure :*

PROMOS *with the* Sheriff, *and their* Officers.

Pro. 'T is strange to think what swarms of unthrifts live
Within this town, by rapine, spoil, and theft,
That, were it not that justice oft them grieve,
The just man's goods by rufflers should be reft.
At this our 'size are thirty judg'd to die,
Whose falls I see their fellows smally fear,
So that the way is, by severity
Such wicked weeds even by the roots to tear.
Wherefore, sheriff, execute with speedy pace
The damned wights, to cut off hope of grace.
Sher. It shall be done.
Cass. [*to herself.*] O cruel words! they make my heart to bleed:
Now, now I must this doom seek to revoke,
Lest grace come short when starved is the steed.—
[*Kneeling, speaks to Promos.*
Most mighty lord, a worthy judge, thy judgment sharp abate;
Vail thou thine ears to hear the 'plaint that wretched I relate.
Behold the woeful sister here of poor Andrugio,
Whom though that law awardeth death, yet mercy do him show.
Weigh his young years, the force of love which forced his amiss,
Weigh, weigh that marriage works amends for what committed is.
He hath defil'd no nuptial bed, nor forced rape hath mov'd;
He fell through love who never meant but wife the wight he lov'd:
And wantons sure to keep in awe these statutes first were made,
Or none but lustful lechers should with rig'rous law be paid.
And yet to add intent thereto is far from my pretence;
I sue with tears to win him grace that sorrows his offence.
Wherefore herein, renowned lord, justice with pity pays;
Which two, in equal balance weigh'd, to heaven your fame will raise.
Pro. Cassandra, leave off thy bootless suit; by law he hath been tried—
Law found his fault, law judg'd him death.
Cass.   Yet this may be replied:
That law a mischief oft permits to keep due form of law—
That law small faults, with greatest dooms, to keep men still in awe.
Yet kings, or such as execute regal authority,
If 'mends be made, may over-rule the force of law with mercy.
Here is no wilful murder wrought which asketh blood again;
Andrugio's fault may valued be, marriage wipes out his stain.
Pro. Fair dame, I see the natural zeal thou bear'st to Andrugio,
And for thy sake (not his desert) this favour will I show:
I will reprieve him yet a while, and on the matter pause;
To-morrow you shall licence have afresh to plead his cause.
Sheriff, execute my charge, but stay Andrugio
Until that you in this behalf more of my pleasure know.
Sher. I will perform your will.
Cass. O most worthy magistrate, myself thy thrall I bind,
Even for this little light'ning hope which at thy hands I find.
Now will I go and comfort him which hangs 'twixt death and life.   [*Exit.*
Pro. Happy is the man that enjoys the love of such a wife!
I do protest her modest words hath wrought in me amaze.
Though she be fair, she is not deck'd with garish shows for gaze:
Her beauty lures, her looks cut off fond suits with chaste disdain:
O God, I feel a sudden change that doth my freedom chain!
What didst thou say? Fie, Promos, fie! of her avoid the thought:
And so I will; my other cares will cure what love has wrought.
Come away.   [*Exeunt.*

ACT I.

DRAMATIS PERSONÆ.—The following list (cf. *Oth.* p. 153) is given in the folio at the end of the play, p. 84 :

The Scene Vienna.

The names of all the Actors.

Vincentio : the Duke.
Angelo, the Deputie.
Escalus, an ancient Lord.
Claudio, a yong Gentleman.
Lucio, a fantastique.
2. *Other like Gentlemen.*
Prouost.

Thomas.
Peter. } 2. *Friers.*
Elbow, a simple Constable.
Froth, a foolish Gentleman.
Clowne.
Abhorson, an Executioner.
Barnardine, a dissolute prisoner
Isabella, sister to Claudio.
Mariana, betrothed to Angelo.
Iuliet, beloued of Claudio.
Francisca, a Nun.
Mistris Ouer-don, a Bawd.

SCENE I.—5. *Put to know.* "Compelled to acknowledge" (Steevens). Cf. *2 Hen. VI.* iii. 1. 43 : "had I first been put to speak my mind ;" and *Cymb.* ii. 3. 110 : "You put me to forget a lady's manners." Pope changed *put* to "not," and the Coll. MS. has "apt."

6. *Lists.* "Bounds, limits" (Johnson). Cf. *Oth.* iv. 1. 76 : "Confine yourself within a patient list ;" and see also *Ham.* p. 249.

7, 8. *No more remains But that*, etc. A passage which has perplexed the commentators. The folio reads :

> "Then no more remaines
> But that, to your sufficiency, as your worth is able,
> And let them worke :"

Theo. conjectured that something had been lost, and attempted to supply it thus :

> "But that to your sufficiency you add
> Due diligency as your worth is able."

Hanmer gave :

> "But that to your sufficiency you join
> A will to serve us as your worth is able ;"

and Tyrwhitt conjectured :

> "But that to your sufficiency you put
> A zeal as willing as your worth is able."

Sundry other ways of filling the supposed gap have been proposed, but these will serve as samples. Others have assumed that the passage is not defective but corrupt, and have tried to emend it by reading "But that to your sufficiencies your worth is abled" (Johnson) ; "But your sufficiency as worth is able" (Farmer) ; "But thereto your sufficiency," etc. (Sr.) ; "But add to your sufficiency your worth, And let," etc. (Coll. MS.) ; "But t' add to your sufficiency" (H.), and so on. The pointing in the text is due to W., who takes *that* to be the demonstrative referring to *science*, and *remains* to be =is wanting. The meaning then is : "then, as your worth is able [that is, your high character rendering you competent], no more is wanting to complete your capacity for the fulfilment of your trust but that [that is, that knowledge of government of which I have just spoken] ; and let them [that is, that knowledge and your worth] work together." If *that* does not refer to *science*, it may refer, as V. suggests, "to the commission, which the Duke must have in his hand, or before him," as is evident from 13 just below. St. explains *that* in the same way, and would read :

> "But that [*tendering his commission*] to your sufficiency,
> And, as your worth is able, let them work."

Clarke finds the antecedent of *that* in *strength* = "the governing power embodied in the *commission* he gives him." Any one of these interpretations of the original text is to be preferred to any of the proposed emendations.

10. *Terms.* "The technical language of the courts. An old book called *Les Termes de la Ley* (written in Henry the Eighth's time) was in Shakespeare's days, and is now, the accidence of young students in the law " (Blackstone).

11. *Pregnant.* Ready. Cf. *T. and C.* iv. 4. 90 : "most prompt and pregnant." See also *Lear*, p. 198.

16. *What figure of us*, etc. How do you think he will *represent* or *personate* us ?

17. *With special soul.* This expression has troubled some of the critics, and " roll " (Warb.) and " seal " (Johnson) have been suggested in its place. Of course it is = with special preference, *soul* being used as *heart* often is. Steevens compares *Temp.* iii. 1. 44 :

> "for several virtues
> Have I lik'd several women, never any
> With so full soul," etc.

20. *Deputation.* Deputyship, viceregency.

27. *Character.* In its original sense of writing ; as in i. 2. 145 and v. 1. 11 below. Johnson asks, " What is there peculiar in this, that a man's *life* informs the observer of his *history* ?" and conjectures " look " for *life*. Mason thought that *character* and *history* should be transposed. Of course, no change is called for, the meaning being simply : in the record of your outward life we read your whole history.

29. *Belongings.* " Endowments " (Malone).

30. *So proper.* So personally or peculiarly. Cf. *T. of A.* i. 2. 106 : " What better or properer can we call our own than the riches of our friends ?"

31. *They on thee.* Hanmer "corrected" *they* to " them," and has been followed by many editors. Cf. Gr. 205–216.

33. *For if our virtues*, etc. Theo. quotes Horace's

> " Paulum sepultae distat inertiae
> Celata virtus."

36. *To fine issues.* "For high purposes" (Johnson).

38. *She determines*, etc. "She *requires and allots* to *herself* the same advantages that creditors usually enjoy,—thanks for the endowments she has bestowed, and extraordinary exertions in those whom she hath thus favoured, by way of *interest* for what she has lent" (Malone). For *use* = interest, cf. *Much Ado*, ii. 1. 288 : "He lent it me awhile, and I gave him use for it," etc.

40. *But I do bend my speech*, etc. "I direct my speech to one who is able to teach me how to govern" (Warb.). *My part in him* = my office delegated to him. For *advertise* = instruct, cf. *Hen. VIII.* ii. 4. 178 :

> "Wherein he might the king his lord advertise
> Whether our daughter were legitimate," etc.

The accent in S. is regularly on the penult. Hanmer reads "can in my part me advertise."

42. *Hold therefore, Angelo.* If nothing has been lost here, we must accept Steevens's explanation that this is what the duke says on tendering his commission to him. Johnson explains it : "That is, continue to be Angelo ; hold as thou art." Tyrwhitt thinks that "the duke may be understood to speak of himself : Let me therefore hold, or stop," as if checking himself in a needless exhortation. W. plausibly conjectures "Hold therefore, Angelo, our place and power." Cf. i. 3. 13 below.

43. *In our remove.* In our absence.

44. *Mortality and mercy*, etc. "That is, 'I delegate to thy tongue the power of pronouncing sentence of death, and to thy heart the privilege of exercising mercy.' These are words of great import, and ought to be made clear, as on them depends the chief incident of the play" (Douce).

46. *First in question.* "First called for, first appointed" (Johnson). Schmidt makes it = "first in consideration."

47. *Commission.* Metrically a quadrisyllable. This making two syllables of -*ion* is rare in the middle of a line. To the examples given by Abbott (Gr. 479) we can, however, add the present, with 1 *Hen. IV.* iv. 1. 62 ("division"), 3 *Hen. VI.* i. 1. 133 ("rebellion"), and *Hen. VIII.* ii. 4. 1 ("commission"). Cf. "patient" in 3 *Hen. VI.* i. 1. 215.

51. *Leaven'd.* Well considered ; "not declared as soon as it fell into the imagination, but suffered to work long in the mind" (Johnson). Warb. changed the word to "level'd."

54. *That it prefers itself*, etc. That is, it places itself before the most important business.

56. *Importune.* Always accented on the penult by S. See *Ham.* p. 190.

61. *Bring you.* Escort or accompany you ; as often. See *W. T.* iv. 3. 122, *Hen. V.* ii. 3. 1, etc. Cf. *Gen.* xviii. 16, *Acts*, xxi. 5, 2 *Cor.* i. 16, etc. For the adverbial use of *something*, see Gr. 68.

64. *Your scope.* "Your amplitude of power" (Johnson).

68. *Stage me.* Make a show of myself. For the verb, cf. *A. and C.* iii. 13. 30 and v. 2. 217. On the passage, see p. 10 above.

70. *Aves.* "All-hails" (*Cor.* v. 3. 139), acclamations.

72. *Does affect it.* Is fond of it, or pleased with it.

78. *To look into the bottom of my place.* That is, to know it thoroughly.

SCENE II.—4. *Its.* One of the rare instances of the word in S. Here it will be noted that it is emphatic. Gr. 228.

15. *That prays for peace.* A petition for peace was included in the form of grace then in common use.

Hanmer changes *before* to "after ;" and the Camb. editors remark : "Hanmer's reading is recommended by the fact that in the old forms of grace used in many colleges, and, as we are informed, at the Inns of Court, the prayer for peace comes always after, and never before, meat. But as the mistake may easily have been made by S., or else deliberately put into the mouth of the 1st Gentleman, we have not altered the text."

21. *What, in metre?* K. takes this to refer to the ancient metrical graces arranged to be said or sung. Schmidt thinks it may mean "in a play, on the stage." *Proportion* in the reply may be = "measure," as Warb. explains it, or simply = form, arrangement.

24. *Grace is grace,* etc. "Grace is as immutably grace as his merry antagonist is a *wicked villain.* Difference in religion cannot make a *grace* not to be *grace,* a *prayer* not to be *holy;* as nothing can make a *villain* not to be a *villain*" (Johnson).

27. *There went but a pair of shears between us.* "We are both of the same piece" (Johnson). Malone quotes Marston, *Malcontent,* 1604: "There goes but a pair of shears betwixt an emperor and the son of a bagpiper ; only the dyeing, dressing, pressing, and glossing makes the difference."

32. *Had as lief.* Good English then as now. See *A. Y. L.* p. 139.

33. *Piled.* "A quibble between *piled*=peeled, stripped of hair, bald (from the French disease) and *piled* as applied to velvet, *three-piled* velvet meaning the finest and costliest kind" (D.).

37. *Forget to drink after thee.* That is, lest I catch the disease in that way.

39. *Done myself wrong.* "Put myself in the wrong" (J. H.).

44. *I have purchased,* etc. I have acquired or got, etc. Cf. *A. Y. L.* p. 177.

The folio continues this speech to Lucio, but the context shows that it belongs to the 1st gentleman, to whom Pope transferred it.

48. *Dolours.* For the play on *dollars,* cf. *Temp.* ii. 1. 17 and *Lear,* ii. 4. 54.

50. *A French crown.* A common expression for a bald head, being a kindred joke to that in 33 above. Cf. *M. N. D.* i. 2. 99: "Some of your French crowns have no hair at all," etc.

54. *Thy bones are hollow.* Steevens quotes *T. of A.* iv. 3. 152 :

> "Consumptions sow
> In hollow bones of man."

78. *The sweat.* The plague, which was popularly known as "the sweating sickness." See p. 10 above.

88. *Houses in the suburbs.* Houses of ill-fame were chiefly in the suburbs.

104. *Thomas.* A name commonly applied to tapsters, probably for the sake of the alliteration.

108. *Enter* PROVOST, etc. The folio begins a new scene, "Scæna Tertia," here, and is followed by some modern eds.; but there is evidently no change of scene. The Coll. MS. omits the name of *Juliet* here; but the preceding line indicates that she is on the stage. Possibly, however, as H. suggests, "Pompey may be supposed to see her just as the others are entering and she is parting from them." It is evident from 137 below that she is not within hearing, nor near the speaker. The Camb. editors suppose that she was "following at a distance behind, in her anxiety for the fate of her lover." At the end of the play she appears again without saying any thing.

114. *The words of heaven,* etc. Some editors adopt the conjecture of Roberts, "The sword of heaven;" but we accept Henley's explanation of the original text: "*Authority,* being absolute in Angelo, is finely styled by Claudio *the demi-god.* To this uncontrollable power the poet applies a passage from *St. Paul to the Romans,* ix. 15, 18, which he properly styles *the words of heaven:* 'for he saith to Moses, I will have mercy on whom I will have mercy,' etc.; and again: 'Therefore hath he mercy on whom he will have mercy,' etc."

119. *Scope.* Liberty, license; as in i. 3. 35 below.

121. *Ravin down.* Ravenously devour. Cf. *Macb.* ii. 4. 28:

> "Thriftless ambition, that will ravin up
> Thine own life's means!"

and *Cymb.* i. 6. 49: "ravining first the lamb." Note also the adjective in *A. W.* iii. 2. 120: "the ravin lion."

Their proper bane = their own poison or destruction. Cf. *Temp.* iii. 3. 60: "Their proper selves," etc.

122. *A thirsty evil.* In Sir William Davenant's *Law against Lovers,* which is founded on this play and *Much Ado,* this is changed to "An evil thirst."

125. *Morality.* The folios misprint "mortality;" corrected by Rowe (after Davenant).

135. *Contract.* Accented by S. on the first or second syllable, as suits the measure. Cf. *Temp.* iv. 1. 84: "A contract of true love to celebrate," etc.

136. *Possession.* H. makes this word a quadrisyllable (see on i. 1. 47 above), and the line an Alexandrine; but it is clearly better to consider it an ordinary line of five feet, with extra syllables which are easily slurred in pronunciation. Cf. the preceding line and 138 just below.

138. *Denunciation.* Proclamation, declaration; the only instance of the word in S. The Coll. MS. changes it to "pronunciation," but, as W. remarks, this only shows the incompetence and the want of authority of the corrector, and, perhaps, the lateness of his labours. Minsheu, 1617, has "To denounce or declare," and Cooper, 1578, "*Denuntiare,*—to shew or tell to another, to give knowledge, to signifie, to denounce," etc.

140. *Propagation.* The reading of the later folios; the 1st has "propo-
gation." Malone conjectures "prorogation," and Jackson "procuration."
W. reads "preservation." A writer in the *Edin. Mag.,* Nov. 1786, thinks
that *propagation* may be from the Italian *pagare,* to pay, and=payment ;
but this is improbable. It is more likely=continuing, keeping up. The
dowry would appear to have been in some way dependent on *her friends'*
approval of her chosen husband, and the couple wanted to keep up their
hold upon it until they had managed to gain the favour of those in charge
of it. For the use of *propagate,* cf. Chapman, *Odyssey,* xvi. (quoted by
Steevens) :

> "to try if we,
> Alone, may propagate to victory
> Our bold encounters;"

and again, *Iliad,* iv. :

> "I doubt not but this night
> Even to the fleete to propagate the Greeks' unturned flight."

J. H. thinks that *for propagation* means "that she might continue to receive the interest." He assumes that Julietta was to receive the interest
while unmarried, and the principal when married to a man approved by
her friends.

148. *The fault and glimpse.* "The faulty glimpse : a fault arising from
the mind being dazzled by a *novel* authority of which the new governor
has yet had only a *glimpse,* has yet taken only a hasty survey " (Malone).
Johnson conjectured "flash " for *fault,* or that we should read "fault *or*
glimpse."

155. *Stagger.* Waver, am perplexed.

156. *Awakes me.* For the *me,* see Gr. 220.

157. *Like unscour'd armour.* Steevens quotes *T. and C.* iii. 3. 152 :

> "Quite out of fashion, like a rusty mail,
> In monumental mockery."

158. *Nineteen zodiacs.* Nineteen circuits of the sun, or years. Whal-
ley would change *nineteen* to "fourteen," on account of i. 3. 21 ; just as
there Theo. reads "nineteen " for *fourteen.* Clarke remarks : "It is
most characteristic that a young fellow like Claudio should carelessly
mention *somewhere about* the period in question, while the staid duke
cites it exactly." It may, however, be one of the poet's little slips in
numbers. Cf. *C. of E.* p. 148 (note on *Thirty-three years*), or *T. of S.* p.
128 (on *This seven*).

159. *Worn.* Put in use ; suggested by the simile of the *armour.*

162. *Tickle.* Ticklish, precarious. Cf. 2 *Hen. VI.* i. 1. 216 : "on a
tickle point."

168. *Receive her approbation.* Enter upon her *probation* (cf. v. 1. 72 below), or novitiate. Malone quotes *The Merry Devil of Edmonton,* 1608 :

> "Madam, for a twelvemonth's approbation
> We mean to make the trial of our child."

170. *In my voice.* In my name ; as in *A. Y. L.* ii. 4. 87 : "And in my
voice most welcome shall you be."

173. *Prone.* Variously explained by the editors : " prompt, ready "
(Nares and H.) ; "significant, expressive " (Malone) ; " humble " (Stec·
vens and W.) ; " deferential, gently submissive and supplicatory "
(Clarke) ; " affectionate " (J. H.), etc. We are inclined to agree with
Steevens and Clarke. Davenant changes the word to "sweet ;" which,
as Steevens remarks, shows, like other of his alterations, " that what appear difficulties to us were difficulties to him, who, living nearer the time
of S., might be supposed to have understood his language more inti-
mately."

174. *Move.* The folio reading ; changed by Rowe to "moves." Capell changes *beside* to " besides."

178. *Grievous imposition.* " Under grievous *penalties imposed* " (Johnson).

179. *Who.* Often = which. Gr. 264. Hanmer and W. read "which."

180. *Tick-tack.* A sort of backgammon (Fr. *tric-trac*).

SCENE III. — 2. *Dribbling.* Weak, ineffectual. Possibly the word
should be *dribbing*, as *dribber*, according to Steevens, was a term of
contempt in archery.

3. *Complete.* Accented on the first syllable because coming *before* the
noun. Cf. *L. L. L.* i. 1. 137 : "A maid of grace and complete majesty ;"
Rich. III. iv. 4. 189 : "Than all the complete armour that thou wear'st,"
etc. See, on the other hand, *T. G. of V.* ii. 4. 73 : "He is complete in
feature and mind ;" *K. John,* ii. 1. 433 : "Is the young Dauphin every
way complete," etc. For many examples of this changeable accent of
dissyllabic adjectives and participles, see Schmidt, p. 1413 fol. Cf. *Cor.*
p. 255 (on *Divine*), and *Cymb.* p. 174 (on *Supreme*).

8. *The life remov'd.* "A life of retirement " (Steevens).

10. *Bravery.* Finery, showy dress ; as in *T. of S.* iv. 3. 57 : "With
scarfs and fans and double change of bravery." See also *A. Y. L.* p. 165.
Keeps= dwells ; as it is still used in some parts of this country.

12. *Stricture.* Strictness ; the only instance of the word in S. *Strictness,* which Davenant substitutes, he does not use at all. Warb. would
read "strict ure," *ure* being "an old word for *use,* practice." Steevens
notes that it occurs in *Promos and Cassandra :* "The crafty man oft puts
these wrongs in ure."

20. *Steeds.* The folios have "weedes ;" corrected by Theo. Walker
conjectures "wills." In the next line, the folios have "slip " for *sleep,*
which is Davenant's word. Cf. ii. 2. 90 below.

21. *This fourteen.* Changed by Theo. to "these nineteen." See on
i. 2. 158 above. For *this* with a plural, cf. *Much Ado,* iii. 3. 134 : "this
seven year," etc. Gr. 87.

27. *Becomes.* Not in the folio ; inserted by Pope.

30. *Quite athwart.* Cf. 1 *Hen. IV.* 1. 1. 36 :

> "when all athwart there came
> A post from Wales loaden with heavy news."

35. *Sith.* Since ; as in iv. 1. 73 below. See *Ham.* pp. 201, 246, 253,
or Gr. 132.

38. *Permissive.* The only instance of the word in S.

42. *And yet my nature never in the fight.* And yet I myself never appearing in the fight. Pope changed *fight* to "sight;" but *strike home* and *ambush* favour its retention as carrying out the metaphor of a contest or struggle.

43. *To do me slander.* The folios have "To do in slander." Hanmer reads "To do it slander;" and there is not much choice between that and the reading in the text, which is Halliwell's. Steevens, in support of Hanmer's, cites 1 *Hen. IV.* iv. 3. 8: "Do me no slander, Douglas." The Coll. MS. has "sight To draw on slander." Sr. conjectures "right To do him slander;" D. "light To do it slander;" and St. "win the fight To die in slander."

The meaning of the whole passage is thus put by Clarke: "Angelo may, under cover of my name, enforce the law, while I take no part in the exertion that is opposed to my nature, and might bring me blame." Clarke reads "do it slander," *it* referring of course to *nature;* and the sense is obviously the same whether we read *it* or *me.*

47. *Bear me.* Bear or conduct myself. The folio omits *me,* which Capell supplied. Pope reads "my person bear."

51. *Stands at a guard with.* Is on his guard against; or "stands cautiously on his defence" (Mason). Johnson makes it ="stands on terms of defiance."

SCENE IV.—5. *Votarists.* For the feminine use, cf. *Oth.* iv. 2. 190. In *T. of A.* iv. 3. 27, Pope reads "Upon the sister votarists," etc.

17. *Stead.* Help, be of service to; as in *M. of V.* i. 3. 7: "May you stead me?" Cf. *Oth.* p. 169.

27. *For that which.* Malone conjectured "That for which;" but the preposition is often omitted in the relative clause when it has been used with the antecedent. Cf. ii. 1. 15 and ii. 2. 119 below. See also Gr. 394.

30. *Make me not your story.* Make me not your subject of mirth, or your jest. Cf. *M. W.* v. 5. 170: "I am your theme" (that is, the subject of your jests, your laughing-stock). The commentators have needlessly tinkered the passage. Malone reads "Mock me not;—your story;" the Coll. MS. changes *story* to "scorn," and Sr. to "sport."

32. *The lapwing.* The bird builds its nest on the ground, and diverts attention from it by running or flying to a distance and attracting the sportsman thither by fluttering and crying. Cf. *C. of E.* iv. 2. 27:

> "Far from her nest the lapwing cries away;
> My heart prays for him, though my tongue do curse."

See our ed. p. 135.

35. *Renouncement.* Renunciation of the world as a nun. S. uses the word only here, *renunciation* not at all.

39. *Fewness and truth.* Briefly and truly. Cf. *in few*=in few words, in *Hen. V.* i. 2. 245, etc. See also iii. 1. 219 below, where it is=in short.

40. *Lover.* For the feminine use, cf. *A. Y. L.* iii. 4. 46, *A. and C.* iv. 14. 101, and *Cymb.* v. 5. 172. The poet's *Lover's Complaint* is the lament of a deserted maiden. Blakeway remarks that the word was used in this

feminine sense long after the time of S., as by Lady Mary Wortley Mon-
tagu in her *Letters*.

42. *Seedness*. A word not found elsewhere. The Coll. MS. has "seed-
ing."

43. *Foison*. Plenty, harvest; as in *Temp*. ii. 1. 163 : "all foison, all
abundance ;" *Id*. iv. 1. 110 ; " Earth's increase, foison plenty," etc.

44. *Tilth*. Tillage ; as in *Temp*. ii. 1. 152, and probably also in iv. 1.
75 below, where the folio has "tithe." For the figure, cf. *Sonn*. 3. 5.

50. *Is*. The Coll. MS. has "who 's."

51. *Bore many gentlemen*, etc. To *bear in hand* was a common phrase
for "keep in expectation, flatter with false hopes." See *Macb*. p. 208.
Johnson wished to read "with hope of action."

54. *Givings-out*. The folio has "giving-out ;" corrected by Rowe.

56. *With full line*. "With the full extent, with the whole length"
(Johnson).

59. *The wanton stings*, etc. Cf. *Oth*. i. 3. 335 : "our raging motions,
our carnal stings."

60. *Rebate*. Make dull (Fr. *rebattre*) ; used by S. nowhere else.

62. *To give fear to use*. "To intimidate *use*, that is, practices long
countenanced by *custom*" (Johnson). Schmidt makes *use and liberty*=
"the practice of liberty, licentious practice."

69. *Grace*. Either "power of gaining favour" (Johnson), or "good
fortune, happiness" (Schmidt); as in *M. N. D*. ii. 2. 89 : "The more my
prayer, the lesser is my grace," etc.

70. *My pith of business*. The pith of my business. Pope omits *pith of*.

72. *Censur'd*. Judged, passed sentence upon ; as in ii. 1. 15, 29 below.
Cf. *Lear*, v. 3. 3 : "That are to censure them," etc.

82. *Freely*. The later folios have "truely."

83. *Would owe them*. Would have them. For *owe*=have, possess, cf.
ii. 4. 123 below.

86. *The mother*. The abbess, or prioress.

88. *Soon at night*. This very night. See 2 *Hen. IV*. p. 204.

ACT II.

SCENE I.—2. *Fear*. Affright ; as in *T. of S*. i. 2. 211 : "Tush, tush !
fear boys with bugs." Cf. *K. John*, p. 147.

6. *Fall*. Generally explained as transitive ; as in *A. Y. L*. iii. 5. 5 :

> " The common executioner,
> Whose heart the accustom'd sight of death makes hard
> Falls not the axe," etc.

It may, however, be intransitive, as J. H. makes it : " Escalus desires that
Angelo and he should act as keen instruments and cut a little, rather than
fall as heavy weights on an offender and crush him to death."

8. *Know*. Reflect, consider.

12. *Blood*. Animal passion ; as in ii. 4. 15, 178, and v. 1. 468 below.
Cf. also *Much Ado*, p. 131, note on *Faith melteth into blood*.

15. *Which.* In which. See on i. 4. 27 above. Hanmer reads "point you censure now in him," Capell "censure him for," and W. "where now."

18. *I not deny.* The transposition of *not* is common. Cf. *Temp.* ii. 1. 121, v. 1. 38, 113, 303, etc. Gr. 305.

22. *What knows the law,* etc. The folio reads "What knowes the Lawes," and some modern eds. give "What know the laws." Malone paraphrases the passage thus: "How can the administrators of the laws take cognizance of what I have just mentioned? How can they know whether the jurymen, who decide on the life or death of thieves, be themselves as criminal as those whom they try?" *Pass on* is of course used in the same sense as in 19 just above.

23. *Pregnant.* Full of probability, evident. Cf. *Cymb.* p. 209, and see also *Lear,* p. 198.

28. *For I have had.* Because I have had, on the ground that I have had. See *M. of V.* p. 134, note on *For he is a Christian.* Gr. 150, 151.

29. *Censure.* Judge, sentence. See on i. 4. 72 above.

31. *And nothing come in partial.* And no partiality be urged or allowed.

39. *Some run from brakes of vice, and answer none.* The folio reads: "Some run from brakes of Ice, and answere none." Rowe gave "through brakes of vice;" and Malone, followed by most of the more recent editors, adopted the *vice.* This seems on the whole the simplest and best emendation, where none is quite satisfactory. *Brakes of vice,* if it be what S. wrote, must mean thickets of vice, with perhaps the double idea of a complication of vices—*many* vices, as opposed to the single *fault* of the next line—and that of thorny entanglements out of which escape would seem difficult. Steevens at first was inclined to read "breaks of ice," and explain the passage "some run away from danger, and stay to answer none of their faults;" but afterwards adopted *brakes of vice,* taking *brakes* to mean "engines of torture," as in Holinshed and other writers of the time. See also Dr. Ingleby's *Shakes. Hermeneutics,* p. 145.

47. *The poor duke's constable.* Cf. *Much Ado,* iii. 5. 22 (Dogberry's speech): "the poor duke's officers."

54. *Precise villains.* He means of course that they are *precisely* or literally villains; but, as Clarke notes, the word gives the impression of "strict, severely moral," as in i. 3. 50 above: "Lord Angelo is precise."

55. *Profanation.* A blunder for *profession.*

57. *This comes off well.* Johnson makes this="this is nimbly spoken, this is volubly uttered;" but it seems rather to mean (ironically, of course) this is well told. Cf. *T. of A.* i. 1. 29: "this comes off well and excellent" (=this is well done).

60. *Out at elbow.* "A hit at the constable's threadbare coat, and at his being startled and put *out* by Angelo's peremptory repetition of his name" (Clarke). Cf. *A. Y. L.* iv. 1. 76: "Very good orators, when they are out, they will spit," etc.

62. *Parcel-bawd.* Part bawd. Cf. *parcel-gilt* in 2 *Hen. IV.* ii. 1. 94, and see our ed. p. 161.

64. *Hot-house.* Bagnio, or bathing-house.

67. *Detest.* Mrs. Quickly makes the same blunder in *M. W.* i. 4. 160 : "but, I detest, an honest maid as ever broke bread."

88. *Stewed prunes.* A favourite dish in such houses. Cf. *M. W.* i. 1. 296, 1 *Hen. IV.* iii. 3. 128, and 2 *Hen. IV.* ii. 4. 159.

91. *China dishes.* These, though not rare in the poet's day, were so costly that it was superfluous to say that they would not be found in common use in a house like Mistress Overdone's.

103. *If you be remembered.* If you recollect. Cf. *A. Y. L.* p. 184.

108. *Wot.* Know ; used only in the present tense and the participle, for which see *W. T.* iii. 2. 77.

114. *Come me.* The *me* is probably the "dativus ethicus," as in i. 2. 156 above and iv. 2. 6 below ; but W. prefers to read "Come we."

123. *A lower chair.* That is, an easy-chair.

The Bunch of Grapes. It was the custom in the time of S., and long after, to give names to particular rooms in taverns. See 1 *Hen. IV.* p. 164, note on *The Half-Moon.*

126. *An open room and good for winter.* The confusion of ideas is sufficiently characteristic of the speaker, but some of the critics have tried to make the passage logical. Talbot makes the preposterous suggestion that *open* is "perhaps from the same root as *oven*, a warm room ;" and the Coll. MS. substitutes "windows " for *winter.*

129. *Russia.* Metrically a trisyllable.

149. *Supposed.* "He means *deposed*" (Malone).

155. *An it like you.* If it please you. Cf. *Hen. V.* iii. prol. 32 : "The offer likes not," etc. Gr. 297.

165. *Justice or Iniquity.* "That is, the constable or the fool. Escalus calls the latter *Iniquity* in allusion to the old *Vice*, a familiar character in the ancient moralities and dumb-shows " (Ritson). Cf. 1 *Hen. IV.* ii. 4. 499 : "that reverend vice, that grey iniquity ;" *Rich. III.* iii. 1. 82 : "like the formal Vice, Iniquity," etc. See also *T. N.* p. 159.

168. *Hannibal.* "Mistaken by the constable for *cannibal*" (Johnson). Cf. 2 *Hen. IV.* ii. 4. 180 (Pistol's speech) : "Compare with Cæsars and with Cannibals."

182. *Thou art to continue.* Elbow evidently takes the "continue " of Escalus to refer to some penalty or other.

196. *Draw you.* "*Draw* has here a cluster of senses. As it refers to the tapster, it signifies *to drain, to empty* ; as it is related to *hang*, it means *to be conveyed to execution on a hurdle.* In Froth's answer, it is the same as *to bring along by some motive or power*" (Johnson). For the play upon *drawing and hanging*, cf. *Much Ado*, iii. 2. 22 and *K. John*, ii. 1. 504.

199. *Drawn in.* That is, taken in, swindled.

203. *Pompey.* As he is called *Thomas* in i. 2. 104, Clarke suggests that *Pompey* was a name given him by waggish customers and adopted by himself ; but it is quite as likely that the *Thomas* was the nickname. See on i. 2. 104 above.

206. *The greatest thing about you.* Probably an allusion to the enormous breeches then worn.

218. *Spay.* The folios have "splay," which some take to be an old form of the word.

229. *Day.* The folios have "bay ;" corrected by Pope. Some retain "bay" because it was an architectural term for a division of a building ; but, as W. asks, "threepence a bay for how long ?" *After*=at the rate of.

235. *Shrewd.* Mischievous, evil. See *J. C.* p. 145, or *Hen. VIII.* p. 202.

239. *But I shall follow it,* etc. St. was the first to mark this as *Aside.*

241. *Jade.* A common term for a worthless nag. See *Hen. V.* p. 170.

247. *Your readiness.* The folios have "the" for *your* (doubtless from confounding y^r and y^e in the MS.) ; corrected by Pope.

Though Elbow says *seven year* and Escalus *seven years,* it must not be supposed that the former is a vulgarism. Cf. *Temp.* i. 2. 53 : "Twelve year since, Miranda, twelve year since," etc. See Mätzner, *Eng. Gram.* vol. i. pp. 230, 240.

262. *Eleven, sir.* Harrison, in his *Description of England* (p. 166 of Mr. Furnivall's ed.), says : "With vs the nobilitie, gentrie, and students, doo ordinarilie go to dinner at eleuen before noone, and to supper at fiue, or betweene fiue and six at afternoone. The merchants dine and sup seldome before twelue at noone, and six at night especiallie in London. The husbandmen dine also at high noone as they call it, and sup at seuen or eight : but out of the tearme in our vniuersities the scholers dine at ten."

SCENE II.—4. *He hath but as offended,* etc. "He hath only, as it were, offended in a dream" (D.). W. reads "offended but as ;" but the transposition, if we regard it as such, is not more peculiar than others in Elizabethan English. See Gr. 422–427.

15. *Groaning.* Cf. *Rich. II.* v. 2. 102 :

> "Hadst thou groan'd for him
> As I have done, thou wouldst be more pitiful."

17. *More fitter.* For double comparatives and superlatives in S., see Gr. 11. Pope reads "more fitting."

19. *Desires.* For the ellipsis of the relative, see Gr. 244.

25. *Save your honour !* The Camb. ed. has "God save." Pope filled out the measure by changing *for 't* to "for it."

28. *Please.* If it please. The folio prints "Please."

32. *For which I must not plead,* etc. Hanmer reads "must plead, albeit," and Johnson conjectures "must now plead, but yet." Malone paraphrases the passage thus : "for which I must not plead, but that there is a conflict in my breast betwixt my affection for my brother, which induces me to plead for him, and my regard to virtue, which forbids me to intercede for one guilty of such a crime ; and I find the former more powerful than the latter."

35. *Let it be his fault,* etc. "Let his fault be condemned, or extirpated, but let not my brother himself suffer " (Malone).

40. *Fine the faults.* Here *fine* evidently has the general sense of punish, as in iii. 1. 114 below : "perdurably fin'd." So the noun here =punishment in general ; as in *K. John,* v. 4. 37 :

> "Paying the fine of rated treachery
> Even with a treacherous fine of all your lives."

Stands in record. Is set down in the statute. S. accents the noun *record* on either syllable, as suits the measure. Cf. *Sonn.* 55. 8 with 123. 11, etc.

41. *Severe.* Accented on the first syllable because coming before the noun; as in 1 *Hen. VI.* v. 4. 114 : "It shall be with such strict and severe covenants." On the other hand, see *A. Y. L.* ii. 7. 155 : " With eyes severe and beard of formal cut," etc. See also on i. 3. 3 above.

45. *You are too cold.* "It is noteworthy that Lucio twice reproaches Isabella with coldness ; and this is the impression that more than one critic has received and given of her character. But the restraint that sways her throughout this scene is just the powerful one which deceives imperfectly judging lookers-on into believing a woman of reticence to be a woman wanting in warmth. See how her upright soul—clear in virtuous perception, honest in righteous avowal—allows the *justice* of the case against her brother, though pleading against its severity : 'O just but severe law !' Then, again, consider the natural timidity and reluctance with which a young girl—a modest, pure girl, a girl who has voluntarily commenced her novitiate for the cloistered life of a nun—would enter upon such a subject as she has undertaken to plead for ; a subject hard even to speak of, most hard to advocate " (Clarke).

53. *But might you,* etc. Walker conjectures "But you might." The Camb. ed. puts a period at the end of the sentence.

54. *Remorse.* Pity ; as very often. Cf. v. 1. 100 below ; and see also *Macb.* p. 171.

58. *Back again.* The 1st folio omits *back*, which the 2d supplies. Hanmer changes *Well* to "and." *Well believe this*=" be thoroughly assured of this " (Theo.).

59. *Longs.* Belongs ; but not a contraction of that word. See Schmidt or Wb.
On the passage, see p. 21 above.

73. *That were.* Warb. reads "that are."

76. *Top.* The Coll. MS. has "God." Cf. *Temp.* iii. 1. 38 : "the top of admiration," etc. It has been pointed out that Dante uses the same expression, "Cima di giudicio."

79. *Like man new made.* "In familiar speech, 'You would be quite another man'" (Johnson). Malone explained it thus : "You will then appear as tender-hearted and merciful as the first man was in his days of innocence, immediately after his creation ;" and Holt White thought it meant : "And you, Angelo, will breathe new life into Claudio, as the Creator animated Adam, by breathing into his nostrils the breath of life."

80. *Condemn.* Changed by Rowe to "condemns."

85. *Of season.* When it is in season. Steevens compares *M. W.* iii. 3. 169 : "I warrant you, buck ; and of the season too, it shall appear."

90. *The law hath not been dead,* etc. As Holt White remarks, "Dormiunt aliquando leges, moriuntur nunquam " is a maxim in law.

92. *If the first,* etc. The folio reading, retained by the Camb. editors, Clarke, and K. Pope reads "the first man," Capell "he, the first," the Coll. MS. "the first one," and W. "but the first."

Edict is accented by S. on either syllable, according to the measure.

K

95. *Looks in a glass.* Alluding to the magic mirrors used by conjurers and fortune-tellers. Cf. *Macb.* iv. 1. 119.

98. *Successive.* Here accented on the first syllable. Cf. *successors* in *Hen. VIII.* i. 1. 60. Gr. 492.

99. *Ere.* The folio has "here ;" corrected by Hanmer. Malone reads "where."

107. *And he that suffers.* That is, the first that suffers.

109. *Like a giant.* Alluding to the savage conduct of giants in ancient romances (Steevens).

112. *Pelting.* Paltry ; as in *M. N. D.* ii. 1. 91 : "every pelting river," etc.

116. *Split'st.* The folio has "splits," a euphonic contraction found elsewhere in second persons ending in -*test.* See on iii. 1. 20 below. Gr. 340.

119. *Most assur'd.* For the ellipsis of the *of,* cf. i. 4. 27 and ii. 1. 15 above. Gr. 394.

120. *Glassy essence.* "That essential nature of man which is like glass from its faculty to reflect the image of others in its own, and from its fragility, its liability to injury or destruction " (Clarke).

122. *With our spleens.* If they had our human spleens, they would laugh away their immortal natures, and become mortal like us. The spleen was thought to be the seat of sudden and uncontrollable fits of mirth, as of melancholy or anger.

126. *We cannot weigh our brother,* etc. " *We* mortals, proud and foolish, cannot prevail on our passions to *weigh* or compare *our brother,* a being of like nature and like frailty, *with ourself.* We have different names and different judgments for the same faults committed by persons of different condition " (Johnson). The Coll. MS. has " You " for *We,* and Theo. "yourself" for *ourself ;* but Isabella is speaking in a general way.

132. *Avis'd.* Advised, or aware. Cf. *M. W.* i. 1. 169 : "Be advised, sir " (that is, listen to reason) ; and *Id.* i. 4. 106 : "Are you avised o' that ?" J. H. says : " Lucio means, does Angelo bear that in mind ?" but the expression is probably an indirect compliment to Isabella, like the preceding speeches of Lucio aside to her. It was a common phrase of the time, and = you may be sure of that.

136. *That skins the vice,* etc. Steevens compares *Ham.* iii. 4. 147 : " It will but skin and film the ulcerous place." S. uses the verb *skin* only in these two passages.

142. *Breeds.* Changed by Pope to "bleeds ;" but the meaning is " My sense *breeds* with her sense, that is, new thoughts are stirring in my mind, new conceptions are hatched in my imagination " (Johnson). Douce explains it thus : " Her arguments are enforced with so much good sense as to increase that stock of sense which I already possess."

149. *Fond.* The word often means foolish (cf. v. 1. 105 below), and here is = " foolishly overprized " (Clarke).

Shekels is printed "sickles" in the folios, as in some of the ancient versions of the Bible. The Coll. MS. has "circles," and Coll. conjectures "cycles."

153. *Preserved.* "That is, preserved from the corruption of the world" (Warb.). The good bishop adds that "the metaphor is taken from fruits preserved in sugar ;" but as Boswell says, "surely our author had ' no such stuff in his thoughts.' "

154. *Dedicate.* For the form, cf. 2 *Hen. VI.* v. 2. 37 : "He that is truly dedicate to war," etc.

159. *Where prayers cross.* Johnson complained that he could not understand this; but the meaning seems to be that the *prayer* or desire of his heart (to seduce Isabella) *crosses* or conflicts with hers that his *honour* (the word suggests that sense to his mind) may be safe. This is evident from what he says in reply to her repetition of *Save your honour !* just below. Henley explains the passage thus : "The petition, 'Lead us not into temptation,' is here considered as crossing or intercepting the onward way in which Angelo was going ; this appointment of his for the morrow's meeting being a premeditated exposure of himself to temptation, which it was the general object of prayer to thwart."

163. *Ha !* Omitted by Pope. Some editors make it a line by itself.

164. *It is I,* etc. "I am not corrupted by her, but my own heart, which excites foul desires under the same benign influences that exalt her purity, as the carrion grows putrid by those beams which increase the fragrance of the violet " (Johnson). *With virtuous season* = with the sweet influences of summer and sunshine.

171. *Evils.* Privies ; as in *Hen. VIII.* ii. 1. 67 : "Nor build their evils on the graves of great men." Henley compares 2 *Kings*, x. 27, and adds : " The desecration of edifices devoted to religion, by converting them to the most abject purposes of nature, was an Eastern method of expressing contempt." The Coll. MS. reads "offals."

185. *Ever.* The later folios have "Even." Pope fills out the measure by reading "Even till this very now," and the Coll. MS. by "Even from youth till now."

186. *Fond.* Foolishly doting. When the word in S. expresses fondness in the modern sense, it generally carries the idea of folly (see on 149 above) with it. Cf. i. 3. 23 above ; and see also *M. N. D.* p. 163, note on *Fond pageant.*

SCENE III.—4. *Spirits in prison.* There is an allusion to 1 *Peter*, iii. 19.

10. *Of mine.* He calls her so because she had been placed in his care. Cf. ii. 2. 23 fol. above.

11. *Flames.* The folios have "flawes" or "flaws ;" but it is probably a misprint for *flames*, which Davenant substituted. Cf. *Ham.* iii. 4. 83 :

> "To flaming youth let virtue be as wax,
> And melt in her own fire."

26. *Offenceful.* The 1st folio misprints "offence full."

30. *Lest.* The reading of the 4th folio ; the earlier folios have "least," which Coll. and V. retain.

31. *As that.* For the reason that, because that. Tyrwhitt puts it thus : "lest you repent (not so much of your fault, as it is an evil) as that, etc."

33. *Spare heaven.* "That is, spare to *offend* heaven" (Malone). Pope reads "seek heaven," and the Coll. MS. "serve heaven." Sr. conjectures "appease heaven."

36. *There rest.* "Keep yourself in this temper" (Johnson).

39. *Grace go with you!* D. gives these words to Juliet (Ritson's conjecture).

40. *Law.* The folios have "loue;" corrected by Hanmer. "Neither her love nor its consequences had any effect upon her life; but the law in question, declaring, as we learn in the old tale on which the play is founded, that the man who broke it 'should lose his head, and the woman offender should ever after be infamously noted,' thus *did* respite her 'a life whose very comfort' was 'a dying horror'" (W.). Some editors retain "love," and Tollet explains the passage thus with that reading: "O love, that is injurious in expediting Claudio's death, and that respites me a life which is a burden to me worse than death!"

SCENE IV.—1. On the passage, cf. *Ham.* iii. 3. 38 fol.

2. *Several.* Separate, different; as in *Temp.* iii. 1. 42, *M. W.* iii. 5. 110, etc.

3. *Invention.* Imagination, or "mental activity in general" (Schmidt). Cf. *Much Ado,* pp. 156, 167. Pope changed the word to "intention."

4. *Anchors on Isabel.* For the figure, cf. *Cymb.* v. 5. 393: "Posthumus anchors upon Imogen."

9. *Sear'd.* Coll. says that Lord Ellesmere's copy of the 1st folio has *sear'd,* not "fear'd," which is the reading of other copies. The misprint seems to have been corrected while the book was being printed. Heath conjectured "sear."

11. *With boot.* Giving something to boot; as in *Lear,* v. 3. 301, etc.

12. *For vain.* Idly, to no purpose.

13. *Case.* Covering, outward garb. Cf. *L. C.* 116: "Accomplish'd in himself, not in his case."

15. *Thou art blood.* Pope, for the sake of the measure, reads "thou art but blood," and Malone "thou art still blood."

16. *Good angel.* Mr. Crosby suggests that Angelo here plays upon his own name. The meaning, of course, is: Though we may write good angel on the devil's horn, it is not his proper crest. Hanmer, not seeing this, made it read "Is 't not," and Johnson conjectured "'T is yet."

27. *The general.* The multitude, the populace. Cf. *Ham.* ii. 2. 457: "caviare to the general." See also *J. C.* p. 142. Some of the editors have been in doubt whether *general* or *subject* is the noun here. On the passage, see p. 10 above.

28. *Fondness.* See on ii. 2. 186 above. The Coll. MS. has "path" for *part.*

43. *That hath from nature stolen,* etc. That is, that hath deprived of life, or murdered.

45. *Saucy sweetness.* Impudent self-indulgence. Hanmer changes *sweetness* to "lewdness." Cf. *sweet uncleanness* just below.

47. *Falsely to take away,* etc. "*Falsely* is the same with *dishonestly,*

illegally; so *false* in the next line but one is *illegal, illegitimate*" (Johnson). On the use of *saucy* in S., see *Cymb.* p. 179.

48. *Restrained.* Forbidden. *Means* has been suspected. Steevens conjectures "mints," and Malone "moulds."

56. *Give my body.* That is, to death.

57. *Compell'd.* Accented on the first syllable because preceding the noun. See on i. 3. 3 above.

Malone paraphrases the passage thus: "Actions to which we are compelled, however *numerous,* are not *imputed* to us by heaven as crimes. If you cannot save your brother but by the loss of your chastity, it is not a voluntary but compelled sin, for which you cannot be *accountable ;*" or, more simply, these *compelled sins* may be *counted* as sins, but are not to be *accounted for* as such.

58. *How say you?* What do you say? Cf. v. 1. 273 below: "Say you?"

73. *Nothing of your answer.* Nothing that you must answer for.

75. *Craftily.* The folios have "crafty ;" corrected by Rowe (after Davenant).

76. *Me.* Omitted in the 1st folio, but supplied in the 2d.

79. *Tax.* Accuse, reproach. Cf. *A. Y. L.* p. 164.

These black masks. That is, the masks now generally worn. Cf. *R. and J.* i. 1. 236:

> "These happy masks that kiss fair ladies' brows,
> Being black, put us in mind they hide the fair."

80. *Enshield.* Enshielded, enclosed. For the form, see Gr. 342.

82. *Received.* Taken, understood. Cf. *T. N.* iii. 1. 131 : "one of your receiving" (that is, understanding).

86. *Pain.* Penalty, punishment ; as in the phrase "on pain of death," etc.

89. *As I subscribe not that,* etc. Though I admit not that nor any other except for the sake of argument. The *as* is what Dr. Ingleby (*S. the Man and the Book,* Part I. p. 145) aptly calls "*the conjunction of reminder,*" being employed by S. and his contemporaries to introduce a subsidiary statement, qualifying, or even contradicting, what goes before, which the person addressed is required to take for granted." Cf. *A. and C.* p. 180, note on *Patch a quarrel.*

Schmidt makes *in the loss of question* = "as no better arguments present themselves to my mind, to make the point clear ;" and J. H. explains it "without disowning the right of calling him to answer for his crime." W. points the passage thus:

> "Admit no other way to save his life.
> (As I subscribe not that nor any other)
> But—in the loss of question—that you," etc.

He thinks that "the *but* must not be shut out of the direct construction." Of course it is grammatically required in that construction ; but the irregularity with our pointing is not unlike what we often find in S. when the construction is broken by a parenthesis. Cf. Gr. 415.

94. *All-holding.* The folios have "all-building," which Schmidt explains as "being the **ground** and foundation **of** all." **The** emendation is due to Rowe. Johnson reads "all-binding."

95. *Mean.* S. often **uses** the singular, though oftener **the plural.** Cf. *R. and J.* p. 189.

97. *To let.* Hanmer omits *to.* Cf. Gr. 350.

103. *That longing I 've been*, etc. **The** folio reads "That longing haue bin sicke for," etc. The emendation in the text is Rowe's. Capell reads "**I have**," K. "had," and D. "**long** I had." Delius considers the folio reading an instance of the ellipsis **of the** nominative. Cf. Gr. 401.

111. *Ignomy.* "Ignominy" (the **reading** of the later folios). *Ignomy* is found in the folio in 1 *Hen. IV.* v. 4. **100** and *T. and C.* v. 10. 33. See 1 *Hen. IV.* p. 202. In the present passage *ignominy* perhaps suits the measure **better, though the line would be a** lame one even then.

Malone **remarks that** Davenant's alteration of the passage may prove a reasonably good comment on it :

> "Ignoble ransom no proportion bears
> To pardon freely given."

122. *If not a fedary*, etc. "If he has not one associate in his crime, if no other person own and follow the same criminal courses which you are now pursuing" (Malone). For *fedary* = accomplice, see *Cymb.* p. 188. The word (spelt "feodary" in the later folios) signifies originally a feudal vassal, and Clarke thinks that it here combines that sense with the other, meaning "one who holds by common tenure, and one of the human fraternity." He paraphrases the passage thus : "Unless we are all frail, let my brother die ; if he do not, as one of his human brethren, holding by their common tenure (but simply as he himself alone) possess and succeed to the inheritance of that weakness which you allow is yours as well as all men's." On the whole, this is to be preferred to Malone's exegesis. J. H. puts it more concisely thus : "Otherwise, let my brother die, if instead of being a mere vassal like other men he alone has frailty for his inheritance." Some change *thy* to "this."

127. *Men their creation mar*, etc. Men spoil women by taking advantage of their weakness ; Steevens accepts an explanation given in the *Edin. Rev.* Nov. 1786 : "men debase their nature by taking advantage of such weak pitiful creatures." Clarke combines the two interpretations : "men impair their own natures and injure women by taking advantage of them." Schmidt says : "men spoil women by that which these learn from them." He gives as parallel uses of *profit by* (=be instructed by, learn from) *A. Y. L.* iv. 3. 84 and *T. and C.* v. 1. 16 ; but in both the expression may as well have its ordinary meaning.

130. *Credulous to false prints.* "That is, take any impression" (Warb.). Malone compares *T. N.* ii. 2. 31 :

> "How easy is it for the proper false
> In women's waxen hearts to set their forms!"

139. *I have no tongue but one*, etc. "Isabella answers to his circumlocutory courtship that she has but *one tongue*, she does not understand this new phrase, and desires him to talk his *former language*, that is, to talk as he talked before" (Johnson). Clarke remarks : "The poet's con-

duct of this difficult scene is a marvel of skill, and proves his insight into womanly nature to be little short of miraculous."

145. *I know your virtue*, etc. "I know your virtue assumes an air of licentiousness which is not natural to you, on purpose to try me" (*Edin. Rev.* Nov. 1786); or "in order to draw me on to confess the like" (Clarke).

150. *Seeming, seeming!* "Hypocrisy, hypocrisy; counterfeit virtue" (Johnson).

153. *Aloud.* Pope carried the word to the next line, and some editors omit it.

156. *My vouch against you.* My assertion to the contrary, my denial of your charge.

159. *Smell of calumny.* Steevens sees here "a metaphor from a lamp or candle extinguished in its own grease !"

160. *Race.* "Natural disposition" (Schmidt); as in *Temp.* i. 2. 358:

> "thy vile race,
> Though thou didst learn, had that in 't which good natures
> Could not abide to be with."

Heath misinterprets the passage thus: "And now I give my senses the rein in the race they are now actually running."

162. *Prolixious blushes.* "What Milton [*P. L.* iv. 311] has called 'sweet, reluctant, amorous delay'" (Steevens).

165. *Die the death.* Elsewhere used of a judicial sentence. See *M. N. D.* p. 126, and cf. *Matt.* xv. 4.

168. *Affection.* Impulse, feeling.

172. *Perilous.* Theo. reads "most perilous." Seymour conjectures "these perilous," and Walker "pernicious."

178. *Prompture.* Prompting, incitement; used by S. only here. For *blood,* cf. ii. 1. 12 above.

179. *Mind of honour.* Honourable mind. Steevens compares "mind of love"=loving mind, in *M. of V.* ii. 8. 42.

ACT III.

SCENE I.—5. *Be absolute for death.* Make up your mind fully for death.

10. *That dost*, etc. The reading of the folios, changed by Hanmer to "That do." Even if *that* refers to *influences*, the irregularity would be not unlike many others in S.; but possibly Porson was right in making *breath* the antecedent. W. says that to "make the breath hourly afflict its habitation" is "an absurd result." An asthmatic might not admit this, but all that the duke means is that life itself may become a burden from being at the mercy of the *skyey influences.* Indeed, is not this the meaning with either construction? In the one case the breath is an affliction because servile to the skyey influences; in the other, it is servile to these influences that afflict it.

W. suggests that we should read *influence* both here and in *W. T.* i. 2. 426, as the rhythm seems to require ; "for *influence* was then a word without a plural, and was used, especially when applied to the heavenly bodies (to which service it was then almost set apart) in its radical sense of in-flowing, and then in the singular form, even when all those bodies are spoken of." Cf. Milton, *P. L.* viii. 512, x. 663, *Comus*, 330, 335, etc. Bacon, however, has the plural in *Essay* 9 : "the evill Influences of the Starrs." See also *Job*, xxxviii. 31.

Keep'st. Dwellest ; as in i. 3. 10 above. Cf. *Ham.* p. 199.

11. *Death's fool.* In the ancient "dumb-shows" Death and the Fool were common characters. The latter is made to employ all his tricks in trying to escape from the former, but finally runs into his clutches.

15. *Are nurs'd by baseness.* "Whatever grandeur can display or luxury enjoy is procured by baseness, by offices of which the mind shrinks from the contemplation. All the delicacies of the table may be traced back to the shambles and the dunghill, all magnificence of building was hewn from the quarry, and all the pomp of ornament dug from among the damps and darkness of the mine" (Johnson). Cf. *A. and C.* i. 1. 35 and v. 2. 7.

17. *Worm.* Serpent ; as in *A. and C.* v. 2. 243, 256, etc. For the old notion that the serpent wounds with its forked tongue, cf. *M. N. D.* iii. 2. 72 :

> "An adder did it ; for with doubler tongue
> Than thine, thou serpent, never adder stung."

K. thinks that the worm of the grave is meant in the present passage.

18. *Provok'st.* Dost invoke, or seek. Cf. *Lear*, iv. 4. 13 : "that to provoke in him" (referring to sleep).

19. *Death, which is no more.* Johnson remarks : "I cannot without indignation find S. saying that *death is only sleep*, lengthening out his exhortation by a sentence which in the friar is impious, in the reasoner is foolish, and in the poet trite and vulgar." But, as Malone replies, the poet means only "that the passage from this life to another is easy as sleep ; a position in which there is surely neither folly nor impiety."

20. *Exist'st.* The folio has "exists," for which see on ii. 2. 116 above.

24. *Effects.* Expressions. Johnson wanted to read "affects" (= "affections, passions of mind"). It is not necessary, however, to refer *complexion* to the mind, as he and some other critics do ; it may mean the face as expressive of the shifting emotions within. Cf. *W. T.* i. 2. 381 : "Your chang'd complexions are to me a mirror," etc.

29. *Sire.* The reading of the 4th folio ; the earlier folios have "fire."

31. *Serpigo.* A cutaneous eruption ; mentioned again in *T. and C.* ii. 3. 81. Here the 1st folio has "sapego," the other folios "sarpego."

34. *Dreaming on both.* "This is exquisitely imagined. When we are young, we busy ourselves in forming schemes for succeeding time, and miss the gratifications that are before us ; when we are old, we amuse the languor of age with the recollection of youthful pleasures or performances : so that our life, of which no part is filled with the business of the present time, resembles our dreams after dinner, when the events of the morning are mingled with the designs of the evening" (Johnson).

For *blessed* Johnson conjectured "blasted," and the Coll. MS. has "boasted."

35. *Becomes as aged*, etc. This has been suspected, not without reason, and sundry attempts at emendation have been made : "becomes an indigent" (Hanmer); "becomes assuaged" (Warb.); "becomes engaged" (the conjecture of St.); "becomes enaged" (that of W.); "becomes abased" (that of the Camb. editors), etc. Clarke explains the old text thus : "becomes as if it were aged, carkingly coveting those things that belong to old people—such as riches, experience, etc." J. H. paraphrases it thus : "Thy youth devotes all its freshness, vigour, etc., to make provision for old age ; as if old age were present in youth and then craving sustenance."

36. *Eld.* Cf. *M. W.* iv. 4. 36: "The superstitious, idle-headed eld." In *T. and C.* ii. 2. 104, the modern reading is "Virgins and boys, mid-age and wrinkled eld ;" but the folios have "old" and the quarto "elders."

40. *Moe thousand deaths.* A thousand more deaths. For *moe*, cf. *A. Y. L.* p. 176.

46. *Sir.* Mason thinks this "too courtly" for the friar, who elsewhere addresses Claudio and Isabella as *son* and *daughter*, and conjectures that we should read "son."

52. *Bring me*, etc. The 1st folio reads "Bring them to hear me speak," and the later folios "Bring them to speak." The emendation was suggested by Steevens.

58. *Lieger.* A resident ambassador. Cf. *Cymb.* p. 174. The editors generally follow the folio in spelling the word "leiger." Capell has "ledger." Steevens quotes Leicester's *Commonwealth :* "a special man of that hasty king, who was his ledger, or agent, in London." Wb. gives *lieger* and *leger*.

59. *Appointment.* Equipment, preparation. Cf. *Ham.* p. 253.

67. *Ay, just.* Cf. v. 1. 200 below. See also *Much Ado*, ii. 1. 29, v. 1. 164, etc.

68. *Vastidity.* Vastness, immensity ; used by S. only here. The folios have "Through" for *Though ;* corrected by Pope.

69. *To a determin'd scope.* "A confinement of your mind to one painful idea—to ignominy of which the remembrance can neither be suppressed nor escaped" (Johnson).

74. *Entertain.* Desire to maintain.

78. *And the poor beetle*, etc. "That is, fear is the principal sensation in death, which has no pain ; and the giant, when he dies, feels no greater pain than the beetle " (Douce).

79. *Sufferance.* Suffering ; as in 2 *Hen. IV.* v. 4. 28, *Cor.* i. 1. 22, *Lear*, iii. 6. 113, etc.

81. *Think you I can*, etc. The meaning is not clear, though the editors generally pass the question without comment. We are inclined to think that Schmidt is right in making *from flowery tenderness* = "from a tender woman, 'whose action is no stronger than a flower' (*Sonn.* 65. 4)." Clarke understands that "Claudio asks his sister whether she thinks he can derive courage from a figurative illustration—that of the 'poor beetle.'" H. is doubtful about the meaning, but thinks it may be "Do you

think me so effeminate in soul as to be capable of an unmanly resolution? or, such a milksop as to quail and collapse at the prospect of death?" Heath would make the sentence imperative, and = " Do me the justice to think that I am able to draw a resolution even from this tenderness of youth, which is commonly found to be less easily reconciled to so sudden and harsh a fate ;" but we cannot imagine Claudio applying the expression *flowery tenderness* to himself. It seems to be used with a touch of contempt for the weak girl who thinks that he needs to be nerved up to *resolution* in the face of death, and that *she* can inspire him with it.

87. *Conserve.* Preserve. The only other instance of the word in S. is in *Oth.* iii. 4. 75 : "Conserv'd of maidens' hearts ;" where, by the way, Schmidt would read "with the skilful Conserves," etc.

90. *Follies doth emmew.* "Forces follies to lie in cover, without daring to show themselves" (Johnson). Steevens compares 3 *Hen. VI.* i. 1. 45 :

> "Neither the king nor he that loves him best,
> The proudest he that holds up Lancaster,
> Dares stir a wing, if Warwick shake his bells."

Cf. *R. of L.* 511 : "With trembling fear, as fowl hear falcon's bells." *Emmew* is = *mew* (see *M. N. D.* p. 126) or *mew up* (*Rich. III.* p. 181). A writer in the *Edin. Rev.* Oct. 1872, proposes "enew" (a term in aquatic falconry, meaning to drive the fowl back to the water as a refuge from the hawk), and H. adopts that reading. J. H. says that "a hawk was said to *emmew* a bird when hovering over and wheeling round it, preparatory to seizure." If he has good authority for this use of the word, no emendation is called for.

93. *Priestly.* The 1st folio has "prenzie," both here and in 96 below ; and attempts have been made to explain that word : by comparison with the Scottish *primsie* (= demure, precise), by connecting it with the old Fr. *prin* (= demure), etc. It has not, however, been proved to be English, and is pretty clearly a misprint for *priestly* (Hanmer's emendation), or some other word. The 2d folio has "princely," K. "precise" (the conjecture of Tieck), and St. "rev'rend." "Saintly," "pensive," "primsie," etc., have also been proposed. W. and H. adopt *priestly.*

96. *Guards.* Literally = facings, or trimmings (see *Much Ado,* p. 124), and hence applied to outward appearances. Cf. the use of the verb in *M. of V.* ii. 2. 164 :

> "Give him a livery
> More guarded than his fellows'," etc.

99. *He would give 't thee,* etc. He would allow thee, in consequence of this offence of mine, to go on offending in this way forever. For *still* = ever, cf. iv. 2. 129, v. 1. 406, 467 below. Gr. 69. Hanmer changes *from* to "for."

107. *Has he affections,* etc. "Is he actuated by passions that impel him to transgress the law, at the very moment that he is *enforcing* it against others?" (Malone) *To bite the law by the nose* is rather to treat it with contempt.

110. *The deadly seven.* These were pride, envy, wrath, sloth, covetousness, gluttony, and lechery (Douce).

114. *Perdurably fin'd.* Everlastingly punished. We find *perdurable* in

Hen. V. iv. 5. 7 and *Oth.* i. 3. 343. For *fin'd*, cf. the use of the noun in ii. 2. 40 above.

120. *Delighted.* Accustomed to delight; as Warb. and Johnson explained it. Cf. Gr. 375. "Dilated," "delinquent," "benighted," "delated," etc., have been proposed.

122. *Region.* Changed by Rowe (followed by many editors) to "regions;" but, as Dr. Ingleby contends, *region* is here "used as an abstract, and in the radical sense," and = "restricted place, or confinement." He adds that Carlyle appears so to have understood it ; for in his *Heroes and Hero-Worship* he paraphrases it as "imprisonment of thick-ribbed ice." So just below *thought* (for which Theo. reads "thoughts") is abstract and the object of *imagine*. *Incertain* = unsettled. Dr. Ingleby paraphrases the latter part of the passage thus : "or to be in an infinitely worse case than those who body forth—or render objective—their own lawless and distracted mind."

124. *And blown*, etc. Cf. *Oth.* v. 2. 279 : "Blow me about in winds ! Roast me in sulphur !"

133. *What sin you do*, etc. The following note is from V. : "'One of the most dramatic passages in the present play (says Hazlitt, in his *Characters of Shakespeare's Plays*), is the interview between Claudio and his sister, when she comes to inform him of the conditions on which Angelo will spare his life. What adds to the dramatic beauty of the scene, and the effect of Claudio's passionate attachment to life, is that it immediately follows the duke's lecture to him, in the character of the friar, recommending an absolute indifference to it.' The attempt of Claudio to prove to his sister that the loss of her chastity, upon such an occasion, will be a virtue, is finely characteristic of the profound knowledge Shakespeare possessed of the intricate complexities of the human heart. 'Shakespeare was, in one sense, the least moral of all writers, (says Hazlitt) ; for morality (commonly so called) is made up of antipathies ; and his talent consisted in sympathy with human nature, in all its shapes, degrees, depressions, and elevations. The object of the pedantic moralist is to find out the bad in every thing ; his was to show that "there is some soul of goodness in things evil."' With reference to the representation of such scenes on the stage, Schlegel observes: 'It is certainly to be wished that decency should be observed on all public occasions, and consequently also on the stage ; but even in this it is possible to go too far. That censorious spirit, which scents out impurity in every sally of a bold and vivacious description, is at best but an ambiguous criterion of purity of morals ; and there is frequently concealed under this hypocrisy the consciousness of an impure imagination. The determination to tolerate nothing which has the least reference to the sensual relation between the two sexes may be carried to a pitch extremely oppressive to a dramatic poet, and injurious to the boldness and freedom of his composition. If considerations of such a nature were to be attended to, many of the happiest parts of the plays of Shakespeare—for example, in *Measure for Measure* and *All's Well that Ends Well*—which are handled with a due regard to decency, must be set aside for their impropriety.'"

134. *Dispenses with.* Excuses, pardons. See *C. of E.* p. 117, note on *Can with such wrongs dispense.*

140. *Heaven shield my mother play'd my father fair !* "God grant that thou wert not my father's true son !" (Schmidt). Cf. *R and J.* iv. 1. 41 : "God shield I should disturb devotion !" See also *A. W.* i. 3. 174.

141. *Wilderness.* Wildness. *Slip of wilderness* = wild slip. Steevens quotes *Old Fortunatus*, 1600 : "But I in wilderness totter'd out my youth," etc.

142. *Defiance.* Indignant refusal. Cf. *defy* = refuse, spurn ; as in *K. John*, iii. 4. 23 : "No, I defy all counsel, all redress," etc.

148. *A trade.* "A custom, a practice, an established habit" (Johnson).

160. *Assay.* Trial, test.

165. *Do not satisfy,* etc. "Do not feed your resolution—or sustain your courage — with hopes that are groundless" (Clarke). Schmidt paraphrases it thus : "Do not set yourself at ease, do not gratify yourself, who were just now resolved to die, with false hopes." Hanmer changes *satisfy* to "falsify," and H. to "qualify" (= abate, weaken).

170. *Hold you there.* "There rest" (ii. 3. 36 above), remain in that frame of mind.

176. *In good time.* "À la bonne heure, so be it, very well" (Steevens).

178. *The goodness that is cheap,* etc. "The goodness which, when associated with beauty, is held cheap, does not remain long so associated ; but grace, being the very life of your features, must continue to preserve their beauty" (V.).

183. *How will you,* etc. The Var. of 1821 has "would" for *will ;* not noted in the Camb. ed.

185. *Resolve.* Inform, answer. Cf. *Rich. III.* p. 224.

189. *Discover.* Uncover, expose ; as in *Lear*, ii. 1. 68 : "I threaten'd to discover him," etc.

191. *He made trial of you only.* That is, he will *say* so.

194. *Uprighteously.* "Uprightly" (Pope's reading), righteously ; used by S. only here.

203. *Miscarried.* Was lost. Cf. *M. of V.* ii. 8. 29 : "there miscarried a vessel of our country ;" *Id.* iii. 2. 318 : "my ships have all miscarried," etc.

206. *She should this Angelo,* etc. Pope "corrected" *she* to "her." Cf. Gr. 111.

207. *By oath.* The 1st folio omits *by*, which the 2d supplies.

Nuptial. The plural is not found in the 1st folio. It occurs in the later folios in *Temp.* v. 1. 308, *M. N. D.* i. 1. 125, v. 1. 75 ; and in the quartos in *Oth.* ii. 2. 8. Cf. *Temp.* p. 143.

208. *Limit.* "Appointed time" (Malone).

209. *Wracked.* The only form in the early eds. Cf. *C. of E.* p. 144, note on *Wrack of sea.*

214. *Combinate.* Contracted, betrothed ; the only instance of the word in S.

219. *In few.* In short. See on i. 4. 39 above.

Bestowed her on her own lamentation. "Left her to her sorrows" (Malone).

221. *Tears.* The later folios misprint "ears."

234. *Refer yourself to.* "Have recourse to, betake yourself to " (Steevens).

239. *Stead up your appointment.* That is, keep it in your *stead.* We have already had the verb in i. 4. 17 above.

243. *Foiled.* The early eds. have "scaled," which has been explained as = "weighed," and by others as = "stripped" or "unmasked." We have little hesitation in accepting White's emendation of *foiled.*

252. *Grange.* A solitary farm-house. Cf. *Oth.* i. 1. 106:

> "What tell'st thou me of robbing? This is Venice ;
> My house is not a grange."

SCENE II.—3. *Bastard.* A kind of sweet wine. Cf. 1 *Hen. IV.* ii. 4. 30: "a pint of bastard," etc.

5. *Usuries.* The Coll. MS. has "usances."

8. *Fox and lamb skins.* Capell reads simply "fox-skins," and Mason conjectures "fox on lamb-skins." Clarke remarks : "The passage seems to us to imply, furred (that is, lined with lamb-skin fur inside, and trimmed with fox-skin fur outside) with both kinds of fur, to show that craft (fox-skin), being richer than innocency (lamb-skin), is used for the decoration."

11. *Brother father.* As *friar = frère,* or brother, the duke returns Elbow's blundering address with one in the same vein. Tyrwhitt remarks that the joke would be clearer in French: "Dieu vous benisse, mon père frère.—Et vous aussi, mon frère père."

22. *Eat, array.* The folios have "eat away ;" corrected by Theo. (the conjecture of Bishop).

36. *Free from our faults,* etc. The 1st folio reads : "From our faults, as faults from seeming free."* The 2d folio has "Free from our faults," etc., and Hanmer corrects the latter part of the line as in the text. This restores both rhythm and sense to the line.

37. *Will come to your waist,—a cord, sir.* That is, will come to have a cord round it, as your waist has ; alluding to the hempen cord which the Franciscan friars wore as a girdle.

41. *Is there none of Pygmalion's images,* etc. Have you no women for your customers as fresh and untouched as Pygmalion's statue was when it became a living woman ?

46. *Trot.* A contemptuous epithet, applied in *T. of S.* i. 2. 80 to an old woman. D. and H. adopt Grey's conjecture of "to 't," but as the word in the folio begins with a capital it is not likely to be a misprint for "to 't." Besides, as W. remarks, there could be no more appropriate name for a bawd's assistant.

52. *In the tub.* Alluding to the "powdering-tub " or "sweating-tub," which was a part of the current treatment for the French disease. Cf. *Hen. V.* ii. 1. 79 : "the powdering-tub of infamy," etc.

54. *Unshunned.* "Unshunnable " (*Oth.* iii. 3. 275), inevitable ; used by S. nowhere else.

---

* W. says that the line in the folio is " without an initial capital," but the capital appears both in Staunton's photolithographic fac-simile and Booth's reprint.

63. *Husband.* Alluding to the received etymology of the word—*house-band.* Cf. Wb.

66. *Not the wear.* Not the fashion. Cf. *A. Y. L.* ii. 7. 34: "Motley's the only wear," etc.

72. *Come your ways.* Used some dozen times by S. *Come your way* occurs only in 10 above. So *go your ways* is more common than *go your way.*

93. *Extirp.* Used again in 1 *Hen. VI.* iii. 3. 24. *Extirpate* occurs only in *Temp.* i. 2. 125.

108. *Detected.* Capell reads "detracted." V. remarks: "The use of this word, in the various extracts from old authors, collected by the commentators, shows that its old meaning was (not *suspected*, as some of them say, but) *charged, arraigned, accused.* Thus, in Greenway's *Tacitus* (1622), the Roman senators, who informed against their kindred, are said 'to have *detected* the dearest of their kindred.'"

113. *Use.* Habit; as in *M. of V.* iv. 1. 268, *Ham.* iii. 4. 163, etc.

Clack-dish. A wooden dish used by beggars to collect alms in; so called because they *clacked* the hinged cover to attract attention. Steevens quotes *The Family of Love*, 1608: "Can you think I get my living by a bell and a clack-dish?" and a stage-direction in 2 *Edw. IV.* 1619: "Enter Mrs. Blague, very poorly, begging with her basket and a clap-dish."

117. *An inward.* An intimate friend. Cf. *Rich. III.* iii. 4. 8: "Who is most inward with the royal duke?"

Shy. Demure. Hanmer reads "sly," which may be right; but cf. v. 1. 54, the only other instance of the word in S.

122. *File.* Number, multitude; as in *Cor.* i. 6. 43: "the common file," etc. For *subject*, cf. v. 1. 14 below. See also *Ham.* i. 1. 72, i. 2. 33, etc.

124. *Unweighing.* Inconsiderate, thoughtless. Cf. *unweighed* in *M. W.* ii. 1. 23; like this, the one instance of the word in S.

126. *Helmed.* Conducted, managed; used by S. only here. The same is true of *testimonied* just below.

134. *Dearer.* The folios have "deare" or "dear;" corrected by Hanmer.

147. *Unhurtful.* Another word used by the poet only once. For *opposite*=opponent, cf. *T. N.* iii. 2. 68: "his opposite, the youth;" and see *Id.* iii. 4. 253, 293, etc.

153. *Tun-dish.* Tunnel, or funnel.

154. *Ungenitured.* Schmidt makes the word =impotent; but perhaps it is explained by 95 above.

159. *Untrussing.* Explained by Schmidt as "unpacking;" but more correctly, we think, by D. as "untying the points or tagged laces which attached the hose or breeches to the doublet."

161. *Not past it.* The folios have "now past it;" corrected by Hanmer.

166. *Scape.* Not a contraction of *escape*, being used in prose by Bacon and others. See *Mach.* p. 214, or Wb. s. v.

173. *Forfeit.* Explained by Steevens as a verb (=transgress, offend),

but perhaps an adjective (=liable to penalty), as Schmidt makes it. Cf. ii. 2. 73 above.

174. *Swear.* Hanmer reads "swerve."

181. *Come Philip and Jacob.* That is, the feast of St. Philip and St. James (Latin, *Jacobus*), or May 1st.

197. *From the See.* That is, from Rome. The folios have "Sea;" corrected by Theo.

201. *The dissolution of it.* The death of goodness. The meaning: "Virtue has become so extreme that it must have a speedy *end.* The reference is to the overstrained sanctity and zeal of Angelo" (V.).

202. *And it is as dangerous.* The 1st and 2d folios have a superfluous *as* before *it.*

205. *Security enough,* etc. Alluding to the trouble that a man often gets into by becoming *security* for a friend. Holt White quotes *Prov.* xi. 15.

223. *Is he resolved to die.* He has made up his mind for death.

224. *Your function.* Your priestly duty. The Coll. MS. reads "the due of your function."

228. *Indeed justice.* That is, the very embodiment of justice pure and simple, with no mingling of mercy. Steevens sees a reference to the maxim "Summum jus, summa injuria."

229. *Straitness.* Strictness; the only instance of the word in S.

234. *He who the sword,* etc. We unhesitatingly agree with W. that these poor rhymes are not Shakespeare's, but the "tag" of some one connected with the theatre. "They are entirely superfluous, having no dramatic purpose, and uttering no moral truth that has not had infinitely better utterance before. Their rhythmical expression is entirely inconsistent with their sentiment and with the diction of the serious parts of this play; it was not in Shakespeare to stop the Duke and set him off in this octosyllabic canter upon the same road over which he had paced before with such severe and stately dignity. The lines are a mere succession of couplets, each containing a perfect if not an isolated thought, which is not Shakespeare's manner under any circumstances, and, above all, in such a soliloquy as the Duke's; 'non color, non vultus.' If we will, we must believe that this soliloquy was written by Shakespeare after those in *Hamlet.* Let who will believe it!"

236, 237. *Pattern . . . go.* The meaning seems to be : to be in himself a pattern ; to have grace to stand firm, and virtue to go forward. The Coll. MS. reads "virtue to go." Clarke paraphrases the couplet thus : "Should be in himself a pattern whereby to know how grace ought to bear itself, and how virtue ought to proceed."

243. *My vice.* It has been disputed whether *my* = "of my dukedom" or is used indefinitely. We have no doubt that the latter is the meaning : to weed the vice of another, and let his own grow.

246. *Wade.* The folios have "made," which, as Malone suggested, is probably a misprint for *wade.* Hanmer reads "that likeness shading crimes," and Heath conjectures "such likeness trade in crimes." The Coll. MS. has "Masking practice" for *Making practice.* The Var. of 1821 reads "Mocking, practise."

252. *Despis'd.* W. follows the folio in reading "despised" and "th' disguised."

ACT IV.

SCENE I.—1. *Take, O, take those lips away,* etc. In *The Bloody Brother,* by B. and F., this stanza appears with the addition of the following:

> "Hide, O hide those hills of snow
> Which thy frozen bosom bears,
> On whose tops the pinks that grow
> Are of those that April wears;
> But first **set** my poor heart free,
> Bound in those icy chains by thee."

Both were printed in the spurious edition of Shakespeare's *Poems,* published in 1640; but probably the second is Fletcher's. W. remarks: "The two stanzas in fact will not make one song, except at great violence to both the form and spirit of the first. For that is written so that the music shall repeat the last three syllables of each of the last two lines, which is impossible with the other: they can both be sung to the same music only by suppressing the beautiful and touching repetition in the first; and this was done when it was introduced in *The Bloody Brother.* Besides, the stanza added in that play is palpably addressed to a woman, while this is just as certainly and as clearly, though not just as palpably, addressed to a man. The command to the boy to break off his song is but a dramatic contrivance to procure the effect of an intrusion upon Mariana's solitude." It may be added that the second stanza is poetically inferior to the first; marred as it is by the conceit—quite in the taste of the time, to be sure—in the second couplet, and by "*those* icy chains," which makes a confusion of metaphors, to say nothing of the awkward repetition of *those.* We suspect, however, that Fletcher wrote "these icy chains."

6. *Seals of love,* etc. Steevens compares *Sonn.* 142. 7 :

> "those **lips** of thine,
> That have profan'd their **scarlet ornaments**,
> And seal'd false bonds of love as oft as mine;"

and *V. and A.* 511 : "Pure lips, sweet **seals** in my soft lips imprinted."

10. *I cry you mercy.* I beg your **pardon.** Cf. *M. N. D.* p. 159.

13. *My mirth,* etc. "Though the music soothed my sorrows, it had no tendency to produce light merriment" (Johnson).

18. *Meet.* Hanmer adds "one ;" but cf. *M. W.* ii. 3. 5 : "'T is past the hour, sir, that Sir Hugh promised to meet ;" and *A. Y. L.* v. 2. 129 : "as you love Phebe, meet ; and as I love no woman, I 'll meet."

21. *Constantly.* Firmly.

27. *Circummur'd.* Walled round ; used by S. only here.

29. *Planched.* Planked, made of boards. Steevens quotes Gorges, *Lucan,* 1614 : "The planched floor," etc. We find also *plancher* = plank ; as in Lyly, *Maid's Metamorphosis,* 1600 : "A hollow plancher," etc.

33-35. *There . . . him.* The folio reads :

"There haue I made my promise, vpon the
Heauy midle of the night, to call vpon him."

Various re-arrangements have been proposed, that in the text being
Walker's conjecture, adopted by the Camb. editors, D., and H. D. says
that it was recommended to him by Tennyson in 1844. Delius and St.
print the passage as prose.

Heavy seems here to be = drowsy, sleepy; as in *Temp.* i. 2. 189, 194,
198, *M. N. D.* v. 1. 380, etc. In *Oth.* v. 1. 42 "heavy night" probably
means cloudy or gloomy night. See our ed. p. 205.

39. *Action all of precept.* "Shewing the several turnings of the way
with his hand" (Warb.). Johnson wanted to transpose *action* and *precept.*

41. *Concerning her observance.* Which it concerns her to observe.

43. *Possess'd.* Informed; as in *Much Ado,* v. 1. 290, *M. of V.* i. 3. 65,
etc.

On *my most stay,* cf. 2 *Hen. IV.* iv. 1. 71: "our most quiet," etc.

46. *Stays upon.* Waits for. Cf. *Macb.* i. 3. 148: "stay upon your
leisure," etc.

47. *Borne up.* Arranged, devised.

60. *Are stuck upon thee.* Cf. *A. W.* v. 3. 45: "I stuck my choice upon
her," etc.

61. *Quests.* Spyings. *Contrarious* here is = contradictory, or perhaps
merely = diverse. S. uses the word elsewhere only in 1 *Hen. IV.* v. 1. 52:
"contrarious winds."

62. *Escapes.* Sallies; changed by Pope to "'scapes."

63. *Dreams.* The folio has "dreame;" corrected by Pope.

64. *Rack.* Probably = strain, distort, misrepresent. Cf. *racker* in *L. L.
L.* v. 1. 21: "rackers of orthography."

73. *Sith.* Since. See on i. 3. 35 above.

74. *Flourish.* "Colour, varnish" (Schmidt), or grace.

75. *Tilth 's.* The folios have "Tithes" or "Tythes," and the Camb. ed.
reads "tithe 's." The emendation was suggested by Warb. and is generally adopted. See on i. 4. 44 above.

SCENE II. — 6. *Leave me your snatches.* None of your attempts at
catching me up! For *me,* cf. i. 2. 156 and ii. 1. 114 above.

10. *Gyves.* Fetters.

12. *Unpitied.* "Unmerciful" (Steevens).

21. *Compound.* Make an agreement.

23. *Estimation.* Reputation.

26. *Mystery.* Calling, trade. Cf. *Oth.* p. 199.

30. *A good favour you have.* There is a play upon *favour* = face. See
J. C. p. 131. Cf. *Gen.* xxix. 17, etc.

40. *True man's.* Honest man's; often opposed to *thief.* See *Cymb.*
p. 182.

41. *If it be too little,* etc. The folios give this to "*Clo.*," or Pompey;
but Capell, followed by most of the editors, transfers it to Abhorson. W.
gives the old arrangement without comment. Clarke explains it satis-
factorily thus: "Abhorson states his proof that hanging is a mystery by

L

saying 'Every true man's apparel fits your thief,' and the clown, taking the words out of his mouth, explains them after his own fashion, and ends by saying 'So (in this way, or thus) every true man's apparel fits your thief.' Moreover, the speech is much more in character with the clown's snip-snap style of chop-logic than with Abhorson's manner, which is remarkably curt and bluff."

46. *He doth oftener ask forgiveness*. It was the custom for the executioner to ask forgiveness of the criminal before fulfilling his office. Cf. *A. Y. L.* iii. 5. 3 :

> "The common executioner,
> Whose heart the accustom'd sight of death makes hard,
> Falls not his axe upon the humbled neck
> But first begs pardon."

53. *Yare*.   Ready, apt.   Cf. *A. and C.* iii. 13. 130 :

> "A halter'd neck which does the hangman thank
> For being yare about him."

See also *T. N.* p. 154.

62. *Starkly*.   Stiffly, as if dead ; the only instance of the adverb in S. Cf. the adjective (used only of dead bodies) in 1 *Hen. IV.* v. 3. 42, *R. and J.* iv. 1. 103, and *Cymb.* iv. 2. 209.

70. *Curfew*.   S. transfers the English (and earlier Norman French) curfew bell to Vienna, as he does to Italy in *R. and J.* iv. 4. 4 (cf. *Temp.* v. 1. 40).

71. *They*.   Changed in the Coll. MS. to " There ;" but the duke is expecting both Isabella and the messenger with a reprieve.   Cf. 80 below.

75. *Stroke*.   The metaphor, as Johnson notes, is taken from the stroke of a pen.

78. *Qualify*.   Abate, control.   Cf. *Ham.* iv. 7. 114, *Lear*, i. 2. 176, etc. *Meal'd*.   "Sprinkled, defiled" (Johnson).   Blackstone made it ="mingled, compounded" (Fr. *mêler*).

80. *This being so*.   The case being as it is ; *this* referring, not to what immediately precedes, but to the former part of the speech.

81. *Seldom when*.   Some print "seldom-when ;" but this is unnecessary, *seldom when* being ="'t is seldom when " (it is seldom that) in 2 *Hen. IV.* iv. 4. 79.

83. *Spirit*.   Monosyllabic ; as often.   Gr. 463.

84. *Unsisting*.   Explained by some as =unresting, but probably a misprint.   Rowe reads "unresisting," Hanmer "unresting," and Capell "unshifting."   Steevens conjectures "unlist'ning," Coll. "resisting," Sr. "unwisting," etc.   W. reads "unlisting," which was proposed by Mason, and is as good an emendation as any.   If *unsisting* means "never at rest, always opening" (the definition is due to Blackstone), the word seems out of place when the door *is* at rest.

90. *Happily*.   Haply ; as often in the early editions, but generally changed to *haply* in the modern ones when dissyllabic.   See *T. N.* p. 158, or Gr. 42.

93. *Siege*.   Seat (Fr. *siége*).   Cf. its use (=rank) in *Ham.* iv. 7. 77: "Of the unworthiest siege ;" and *Oth.* i. 2. 22 : "men of royal siege."

95. *Lordship's.* The folios have "lords ;" corrected by Pope. The error probably arose from the use of the contraction " Lord." for *lordship.* In *T. of S.* ind. 2. 2, the folio reads " Wilt please your Lord drink a cup of sacke ?"

96. *And here comes,* etc. The folios give this speech to " *Pro.*," but it evidently belongs to the Duke, as Tyrwhitt conjectured.

105. *His.* Its. Gr. 217, 228.

111. *Putting-on.* Urging, incitement. Cf. *Cor.* ii. 3. 260: " you ne'er had done 't . . . but by our putting on," etc.

122. *What is,* etc. Who is, etc. Cf. 2 *Hen. IV.* i. 2. 66 : " What 's he that goes there ?" Gr. 254.

125. *Nine years old.* Cf. *Ham.* iv. 6. 15 : " Ere we were two days old at sea," etc.

130. *Fact.* Deed, crime. See *W. T.* p. 175.

137. *Insensible of mortality and desperately mortal.* " Insensible of his being subject to death, and desperate in his incurring of death " (Clarke). Schmidt, following Johnson, makes *desperately mortal* = " destined to die without hope of salvation."

149. *In the boldness of my cunning.* " In the confidence of my sagacity " (Steevens).

153. *In a manifested effect.* " That is, so that its being manifest may be the effect or result of my exposition " (Schmidt).

158. *Limited.* Appointed ; as in *Macb.* ii. 3. 56: " my limited service," etc.

165. *Discover the favour.* Recognize the face. Cf. 30 above.

168. *Tie the beard.* *Tie* has been changed to " dye " and " trim ;" but, as Clarke remarks, it is probable that the beard was sometimes tied up out of the way of the axe, at the request of the sufferer. Sir Thomas More, when laying his head on the block, said to the executioner : " Let me put my beard aside ; that hath not committed treason."

169. *Bared.* Referring to the shaving of the head, and perhaps also to the tying of the beard. The first three folios have " bar'de," and the 4th " barb'd."

170. *Fall to you upon this.* Befall you on account of this.

181. *Attempt.* Tempt ; as in *M. of V.* iv. 1. 421 : " I must attempt you further," etc.

183. *Character.* Handwriting.

192. *Is writ.* Hanmer reads " is here writ," which is of course what is meant.

The unfolding star. Steevens quotes Milton, *Comus,* 93 :

> " The star that bids the shepherd fold
> Now the top of heaven doth hold."

196. *Present shrift.* Immediate absolution (after confession). Cf. *R. and J.* ii. 3. 56 : " Riddling confession finds but riddling shrift."

197. *Absolutely resolve you.* " Entirely convince you " (Mason).

SCENE III.—5. *Brown paper.* Rowe changes *paper* to " pepper ;" but Steevens quotes *Michaelmas Term, Com.* 1607: " I know some gentlemen

in town have been glad, and are glad at this time, to take up commodities
in hawk's-hoods and brown paper;" *A New Trick to Cheat the Devil,*
1636:
> "to have been so bit already
> With taking up commodities of brown paper,
> Buttons past fashion, silks and satins,
> Babies and children's fiddles, with like trash
> Took up at a dear rate, and sold for trifles;"

Greene's *Defence of Coney-Catching,* 1592: "so that if he borrow an hundred pound, he shall have forty in silver, and threescore in wares; as
lute-strings, hobby-horses, or brown paper," etc. Farmer and Douce add
many similar passages, illustrating the practice of the money-lenders of
that time. V. remarks: "An amusing and instructive paper might be
made up from the plays, novels, and essays of France and England, for
the last three centuries, describing the still familiar arts of the money-
lenders, to whom men of desperate credit are driven for aid, in contriving
to avoid the usury laws, by obliging the hapless customer to take a portion of their loan in some unsalable commodities, such as 'brown paper
and old ginger.' From Shakespeare, who, as he soon became (in his own
phrase) 'a rich fellow enough, and had every thing handsome about him,'
must have described only the experience of others, to Sheridan, who
doubtless related his own experience in that of Charles Surface, there is
hardly an English writer of comic fiction but has at least hinted at this
fruitful topic. Le Sage, Molière, etc., down to the present novelists of
Paris, have also found in this perpetual food for pleasantry; and their
laughable satire would not require much alteration to make it very intel-
ligible on this side of the Atlantic. The first notice of it that has fallen
in my way was in Wilson's *Discourse on Usury* (1572); and, as he
speaks of it as being then no novelty, this establishes a very respectable
antiquity for this time-honoured usage."

7. *For the old women were all dead.* On the fondness of old women
for *ginger,* cf. *M. of V.* iii. 1. 10: "I would she were as lying a gossip in
that as ever knapped ginger," etc.

10. *Peaches him.* Impeaches him as; an obvious play on *peach-coloured.*

12. *The rapier and dagger man.* See p. 11 above.

14. *Forthright.* The folios have " Forthlight ;" corrected by Warb.
S. uses *forthright* in *Temp.* iii. 3. 3 and *T. and C.* iii. 3. 158. For *Shooty*
(the folios have " Shootie " and " Shooty ") Warb. reads " Shooter " and
some editors "Shoe-tie."

17. *For the Lord's sake.* The cry of debtors in prison in begging alms
of the passers-by. Malone quotes a poem entitled *Paper's Complaint,*
printed about 1611

> "Good gentle writers, for the Lord's sake, for the Lord's sake,
> Like Ludgate prisoner, lo, I, begging, make
> My mone;"

and Nash's *Pierce Pennilesse,* 1593: "crying for the Lord's sake out at
an iron window." The Coll. MS. has "in for the Lord's sake."

32. *I hear his straw rustle.* "The effect of these few words, and of

those immediately preceding, is marvellously strong, though so condensed. They give the impression of the caged wild-beast-man, with the unwillingness of his keepers to enter his den and bring him forth" (Clarke).

37. *Clap into your prayers.* Cf. *A. Y. L.* v. 3. 11: "Shall we clap into 't roundly, without hawking or spitting?" and *Much Ado,* iii. 4. 44: "Clap us into 'Light o' love,'" etc.

61. *O gravel heart!* O flinty heart! The Coll. MS. has "O grovelling beast!" which W. adopts, though Coll. does not.

65. *Transport him.* "Remove him from one world to another" (Johnson).

77. *Whiles.* Used by S. interchangeably with *while,* which Pope substitutes here.

85. *Journal.* Diurnal; as in *Cymb.* iv. 2. 10: "your journal course."

86. *The under generation.* "This lower world" (*Temp.* iii. 3. 54). The folios have "yond" for *under,* which is Hanmer's emendation. Pope reads "yonder." etc. Cf. *Lear,* ii. 2. 170: "Approach, thou beacon to this under world," etc. Steevens takes *the under generation* to be the Antipodes, and cites *Rich. II.* iii. 2. 38 (see our ed. p. 189).

97. *By cold gradation and well-balanc'd form.* That is, coolly and deliberately (not hastily and passionately), and with due regard to form. The folios have "weale-balanc'd" or "weal balanc'd;" corrected by Rowe. Schmidt would retain the old text, making it = "with due observance of all forms, which it would be against the public interest not to observe."

100. *Convenient.* Proper, becoming.

101 *Commune.* Accented by S. on the first syllable, except perhaps in *W. T.* ii. 1. 162.

107. *Make her.* That is, make for her.

108. *When it is least expected.* Johnson remarks: "A better reason might have been given. It was necessary to keep Isabella in ignorance, that she might with more keenness accuse the deputy."

116. *Close.* Silent, or secret.

118. *Shall not.* Will not.

120. *Injurious.* The Coll. MS. has "perjurious." Cf. *Cymb.* p. 187.

126. *Covent.* "Convent" (Rowe's reading). It is an old form of that word, occurring again in *Hen. VIII.* iv. 2. 19. *Covent Garden* in London was originally the garden of the *covent* at Westminster. W. and H. have "convent."

Confessor. Accented by S. on either the first or second syllable, according to the measure.

127. *Instance.* Intimation. Cf. *C. of E.* i. 1. 65:

> "Before the always-wind-obeying deep
> Gave any tragic instance of our harm."

Or *instance* may be = proof (cf. *A. Y. L.* p. 170), referring to what follows.

130, 131. *If you can pace,* etc. The pointing is that suggested by the Camb. editors. The common reading is

> "If you can, pace your wisdom
> In that good path that I would wish it go."

H. has

> "If you can pace your wisdom
> **In that** good path that I would wish it **go,**
> Then you shall have," etc.

132. *Your bosom.* Your heart's desire. Cf. *IV. T.* iv. 4. 574 : "you have your father's bosom there," etc.

141. *Home and home.* Cf. *Ham.* iii. 3. 29 : "she 'll tax him home ;" and see our ed. p. 232.

142. *Combined.* Bound, pledged. Cf. *combinate* in iii. 1. 214 above.

156. *Beholding.* Many of the modern eds. substitute "beholden," which is not found in S. See *M. of V.* p. 135. Gr. 372.

157. *He lives not in them.* "His character depends not on them" (Steevens).

159. *Woodman.* Huntsman (cf. *Cymb.* p. 199), with the equivocal sense which the word had of hunting the *dear* rather than the *deer.* Reed quotes *The Chances,* i. 9 :

> "Well, well, son John,
> I see you are a woodman, and can choose
> Your deer, though it be i' the dark."

169. *Medlar.* The fruit of the *Mespilus Germanica,* a tree still common in England. Cf. *A. Y. L.* iii. 2. 125, 128.

SCENE IV.—1. *Hath disvouched other.* Has contradicted the others. Cf. *J. C.* i. 2. 230 : "every time gentler than other," etc. Gr. 12.

5. *Redeliver.* The 1st folio has "re-liuer," the later folios "deliver." *Redeliver* is due to Capell.

7. *And why should we,* etc. "It is the conscious guilt of Angelo that prompts this question. The reply of Escalus is such as arises from an undisturbed mind, that only considers the mysterious conduct of the duke in a political point of view" (Steevens).

15. *Of sort and suit.* Of rank (cf. *Hen. V.* p. 181, note on *Great sort*) and such as owe attendance. By feudal law, all vassals were bound to be ready at all times to attend and serve their lord ; or, as the expression was, they owed him "suit and service."

18. *Unpregnant.* Unready, unapt for business. Cf. *Ham.* ii. 2. 595 : "unpregnant of my cause ;" and see our ed. p. 213. Cf. also the use of *pregnant* in i. 1. 11 above.

23. *Tongue.* For the verb, cf. *Cymb.* v. 4. 148 :

> "such stuff as madmen
> Tongue and brain not."

Dares her no. "Bids her not dare to do it" (Clarke), or admonishes her not to do it. For the use of *no,* a writer in the *Monthly Review* compares B. and F., *The Chances,* iii. 4 : "I wear a sword to satisfy the world no" (that it is not so) ; and *A Wife for a Month,* iv. : "I am sure he did not, for I charg'd him no" (not to do it). Schmidt thinks the meaning may be "defies her denial of my assertions." Pope omits *no ;* Hanmer reads "dares her : no ;" Capell "dares her? no ;" and W. "dares her on" (the conjecture of Becket).

24. *Bears so credent bulk.* The first three folios read "bears of a credent bulk;" the 4th folio changes "of" to "off." Pope has "bears off all credence," Theo. "bears a credent bulk," the Coll. MS. "bears such a credent bulk," and Sr. "here's of a credent bulk." The emendation in the text is Dyce's, and is adopted by Clarke and H. *Credent bulk* =great credibility, or "weight of credit" (Schmidt).

25. *Particular.* Private, individual. Cf. *Cor.* p. 254.

SCENE V.—1. *These letters.* "Peter never delivers the letters, but tells his story without any credentials. The poet forgot the plot which he had formed" (Johnson).

5. *Blench.* Start away. Cf. *W. T.* i. 2. 333: "Could man so blench?" and see our ed. p. 160.

8. *Valentinus.* The folios have "Valencius," and Pope reads "Unto Valentius." *Valentinus* is Capell's correction.

9. *Trumpets.* Trumpeters; as in *Hen. V.* iv. 2. 61: "I will the banner from a trumpet take," etc.

SCENE VI.—4. *To veil full purpose.* To cover his full intent. Theo. reads "t' availful purpose," and Hanmer "to 'vailful purpose," which H. adopts. Neither *'vailful* nor *availful* is found elsewhere in S.

13. *Generous and gravest.* That is, most generous, or most noble; the superlative inflection really belonging to both adjectives. See Gr. 398. For *generous*, cf. *Oth.* p. 188.

14. *Hent.* Taken possession of, occupied. Cf. *W. T.* iv. 3. 133: "merrily hent the stile-a." See also the noun (=hold, seizure) in *Ham.* iii. 3. 88: "a more horrid hent."

ACT V.

SCENE I.—7. *Yield you forth to.* W. and H. read "yield forth to you." The use of *forth* with *yield* is somewhat peculiar. The expression may be=call you forth to give you public thanks.

8. *Bonds.* Obligations. Cf. *A. W.* p. 144.

14. *Subject.* Used in a collective sense; as in iii. 2. 122 above. Theo. reads "subjects."

20. *Vail your regard.* Bend down your look. Cf. *M. of V.* i. 1. 28: "Vailing her high-top lower than her ribs;" and see our ed. p. 128.

36. *Strange.* The Coll. MS. has "strangely;" but the ellipsis of the adverbial inflection in pairs of adverbs is not unusual in S. Cf. *Rich. II.* i. 3. 3: "sprightfully and bold;" *Rich. III.* iii. 4. 50: "cheerfully and smooth," etc. Gr. 397.

37. *Strange, but yet.* Here also the Coll. MS. "corrects" the poet's English into "strangely yet."

42. *Nay, it is.* Pope omits *it is.*

48. *Conjure.* Accented by S. on either syllable, without regard to the meaning. Cf. *M. N. D.* p. 164. Capell reads "do conjure."

53. *Wicked'st.* For contracted superlatives in S., see Gr. 473.

54. *Absolute.* Complete, perfect. Cf. *Ham.* v. 2. 111 : "an absolute gentleman." See also *Hen. V.* p. 170.

56. *Dressings.* "Semblance of virtue, habiliments of office" (Johnson). *Characts* = characters, in the sense of writing ; here used figuratively = distinctive marks, outward characteristics. Cf. i. 1. 27 above.

63. *As e'er I heard,* etc. That ever I heard, etc. Capell conjectured "ne'er" for *e'er,* and some recent editors have shown their ignorance of Shakespeare's English by adopting that reading. "The oddest frame of sense as e'er I heard" is the leading construction (for which cf. *J. C.* i. 2. 33 : "that gentleness . . . as I was wont to have ;" and see *Id.* i. 2. 174), and line 62 is inserted as a parenthetic explanation of *frame of sense.* Cf. Gr. 112 and 280.

Dr. Bucknill, in his *Psychology of S.* (quoted by Clarke) considers the passage as an instance of the poet's thorough knowledge of the right tests whereby to detect insanity. The duke says that he believes Isabella to be mad, and then adds that her madness has just that strange appearance of sense and connection which sometimes, though rarely, is heard from those who are mad. Then she, dreading lest her eagerness should give an air of disconnection to what she says, bids him "not banish reason for inequality," that is, "not believe her devoid of reason on account of incoherency or inconsistency."

64. *Do not banish reason,* etc. Johnson explains this : "Let not the high quality of my adversary prejudice you against me." Schmidt doubts whether *inequality* means "incongruity, improbability," or "partiality."

67. *And hide the false seems true.* If this be what S. wrote, the meaning must be "and suppress the false which seems true." *Hide* seems not just the word to use in this sense, but, as Malone suggests, it may have been chosen for the sake of the antithesis. Theo. reads "Not hide," the plausible conjecture of Warb.

72. *Probation.* Cf. i. 2. 168 above.

74. *As then.* For *as* with expressions of time, see *Temp.* p. 113, note on *As at that time.* Cf. Gr. 114.

An't like. If it please. Cf. ii. 1. 155 above.

90. *To the matter.* "German to the matter" (*Ham.* v. 2. 165), suited to the case.

94. *Refell'd.* Refuted (Latin *refello*) ; used by S. only here. Pope reads "repell'd."

98. *Concupiscible.* "Concupiscent" (Pope's reading). S. uses the word nowhere else, and *concupiscent* and *concupiscence* not at all. We find the noun *concupy* in *T. and C.* v. 2. 177.

100. *Remorse.* Pity, compassion ; as in ii. 2. 54 above. *Confutes* = prevails over.

104. *Like.* Seeming like truth, likely to be believed. Warb. explained *like* as = "seemly ;" but Johnson is clearly right in taking the speech to be a wish "that since her tale is true it may be believed."

105. *Fond.* Foolish. See on ii. 2. 149 and 186 above.

107. *Practice.* Plotting, conspiracy ; as in 123 below. Cf. *Much Ado,* p. 156, or *Ham.* p. 255.

108. *Imports no reason.* Carries with it no reason, is not reasonable.

110. *Proper to himself.* Belonging to himself. Cf. i. 1. 30 above.

118. *Countenance.* Explained by Warb. as="partial favour;" but it seems rather="false appearance," as Mason makes it. Schmidt puts it under the head of "authority, credit, patronage."

127. *'T is.* Contemptuous; as often. See *A. Y. L.* p. 139.

130. *Swing'd.* Whipped, beaten. Cf. 2 *Hen. IV.* v. 4. 21: "I will have you as soundly swinged for this," etc.

131. *This'.* This is. Cf. *Lear*, p. 246. Here the first three folios have *this'*, and the 4th folio "this." Rowe reads "this is," the Camb. ed. "this 's," and H. "'t is."

142. *Ungot.* Not begotten. Cf. *ungotten* in *Hen. V.* i. 2. 287.

145. *A temporary meddler.* That is, one who meddles with temporal matters, or things not concerning his spiritual profession. It is the only instance of the word in S.

147. *Trust.* The Coll. MS. has "truth."

152. *Mere request.* Particular request. For the use of *mere* and *merely* in S., see *Temp.* p. 111, note on *We are merely cheated*, etc.

157. *Probation.* Proof; as in *Ham.* i. 1. 156 (see our ed. p. 176), *Oth.* iii. 3. 365 (see p. 191), etc.

158. *Convented.* Summoned, called to appear. Cf. *T. N.* p. 169.

160. *Vulgarly.* Before all the people, publicly (Steevens and Schmidt). Some explain it as "grossly, coarsely;" and Clarke thinks it combines both meanings.

166. *Impartial.* Taking no part; as in *V. and A.* 748: "the impartial gazer." Theo. reads "I will be partial." Malone shows that *impartial* was sometimes used in the sense of *partial;* but there is no necessity for explaining it so here.

168. *Her face.* The reading of the 2d folio; the 1st has "your face."

200. *Just.* See on iii. 1. 67 above.

203. *Abuse.* Deception, or delusion. Cf. *Ham.* p. 255.

210. *Garden-house.* Summer-house; often, as Malone shows by quotations from contemporaneous writers, the scene of intrigue.

217. *Her promised proportions,* etc. "Her fortune, which was promised *proportionate* to mine, fell short of the *composition*, that is, contract or bargain" (Johnson). *Proportion*, however, may be simply=portion; as in *T. G. of V.* ii. 3. 3: "I have received my proportion." See also *Per.* iv. 2. 29.

219. *Disvalued.* Depreciated; the only instance of the word in S.

221. *Spake.* For the past tense after *since*, see Gr. 132, 347.

230. *Confixed.* Fixed; used by S. nowhere else.

234. *Informal.* Insane; as *formal* was=sane. Cf. *C. of E.* v. 1. 105: "To make of him a formal man again;" and see our ed. p. 144. S. uses *informal* only here.

235. *More mightier.* For double comparatives and superlatives in S., see Gr. 11.

237. *Practice.* Plot, conspiracy; as in 107 and 123 above.

238. *To your height of pleasure.* As much as you please. Pope reads "unto" for *to*, and Capell "even to."

240. *Compact.* Leagued, united in conspiracy; as in *Lear*, ii. 2. 125:

> "When he, compact, and flattering his displeasure,
> Tripp'd me behind."

243. *Seal'd in approbation.* "*Approved*, and *sealed* in testimony of that *approbation*, and, like other things so sealed, no more to be called in question" (Johnson).

253. *To hear this matter forth.* "To hear the further process of the matter" (Schmidt); or "hear it to the end" (Johnson).

258. *Throughly.* Thoroughly. See *M. of V.* p. 144, note on *Throughfares.*

261. *Cucullus non facit monachum.* "All hoods make not monks," as it is translated in *Hen. VIII.* iii. 1. 23. The Latin is quoted again in *T. N.* i. 5. 62.

265. *Enforce.* Urge, give the weight of your testimony concerning.

278. *Light.* A word on which S. is fond of quibbling. Cf. *M. of V.* v. 1. 129:

> "Let me give light, but let me not be light,
> For a light wife doth make a heavy husband."

See also *Id.* ii. 6. 42, iii. 2. 91, *L. L. L.* v. 2. 26, etc.

290. *Respect to your great place!* etc. This seems to be spoken with a touch of irony. Malone suspected that a line had been lost before this; but the connection is clear enough: yes, I know where I am, and the respect due to your *office* at least.

299. *Retort your manifest appeal.* "To *refer back* to Angelo the cause in which you *appealed* from Angelo to the duke" (Johnson). Schmidt makes *retort*=reject.

306. *His proper ear.* His own ear. See on i. 2. 114 above.

309. *Touze.* Pull, tear. See *W. T.* p. 206.

314. *Nor here provincial.* Nor under the jurisdiction of this ecclesiastical province (Malone and Schmidt).

317. *The stew.* Apparently=the cauldron; with perhaps an allusion to *stew* = brothel, as H. suggests. Steevens compares *Macb.* iv. 1. 19: "Like a hell-broth boil and bubble."

319. *The forfeits in a barber's shop.* "Those shops were places of great resort, for passing away time in an idle manner. By way of enforcing some kind of regularity, and perhaps at least as much to promote drinking, certain laws were usually hung up, the transgression of which was to be punished by specific forfeitures. It is not to be wondered that laws of that nature were as often laughed at as obeyed" (Nares). Dr. Kenrick has given some specimens of these *forfeits*—as, for instance,

> "Who rudely takes another's turn
> A forfeit mug may manners learn;"

and

> "Who checks the barber in his tale
> Must pay for each his pot of ale."

According to Steevens, these are forgeries, but St. thinks they may be authentic. Henley remembered to have seen such *forfeits* in Devonshire (printed like "King Charles's Rules"), but could not recollect any of them.

339. *Close.* Come to an agreement, make his peace. Elsewhere it is followed by *with*, but the sense is the same. Cf. *W. T.* iv. 4. 830, *J. C.* iii. 1. 202, 2 *Hen. IV.* ii. 4. 354, etc. The Coll. MS. has "gloze."

344. *Giglots.* Wantons; spelt "giglets" in the old editions. Cf. the adjective in 1 *Hen. VI.* iv. 7. 41 : "giglot wench ;" and *Cymb.* iii. 1. 31 : "O giglot fortune !"

345. *Companion.* Used contemptuously (= fellow) ; as in *J. C.* iv. 3. 138 : "Companion, hence !" 2 *Hen. IV.* ii. 4. 132 : "I scorn you, scurvy companion," etc. See *Temp.* p. 131, note on *Your fellow.*

351. *Sheep-biting.* Explained by Schmidt as "morose, surly, malicious ;" but according to D. it was a cant term for thieving. Cf. *sheep-biter* in *T. N.* ii. 5. 6, and see our ed. p. 142.

Be hanged an hour! This seems to have been a cant phrase ; but Hanmer reads "hanged ! An hour ?" and Johnson conjectures "hanged —an' how ?" Lloyd suggests "hanged anon."

360. *Do thee office.* "Do thee service" (Steevens).

366. *My passes.* My proceedings, or acts ; used like *passages* in *T. N.* iii. 2. 77, 1 *Hen. IV.* iii. 2. 8, etc.

374. *Which consummate.* Which being consummated. For the form, cf. *dedicate* in ii. 2. 154 above.

379. *Advertising and holy.* "Attentive and faithful" (Johnson). *Advertising* is rather=counselling, instructing ; as in i. 1. 41 above. *Holy* apparently refers to his having acted the part of a priest.

382. *Pain'd.* Made labour and trouble for. Cf. *painful*=laborious, in *Temp.* iii. 1. 1, *L. L. L.* ii. 1. 23, etc.

384. *Free.* Liberal, generous.

388. *Remonstrance.* "Demonstration, manifestation" (Schmidt) ; the only instance of the word in S. Malone conjectured "demonstrance," which St. adopts ; but *remonstrance* unquestionably had that sense in the poet's day. H. cites an example of it from Hooker.

392. *Brain'd my purpose.* "Knocked my design on the head" (Johnson).

397. *Salt.* Lustful ; as in *A. and C.* ii. 1. 21 : "salt Cleopatra," etc.

401. *Of promise-breach.* Hanmer reads "in promise-breach ;" but the "confusion of construction" is not unlike others in S. Cf. Gr. 415.

404. *His proper tongue.* His own tongue. Cf. 306 above.

407. *Quit.* Requite ; as in 492 below. Cf. *Rich. II.* p. 208.

408. *Fault 's.* D. reads "fault," making the next line parenthetical.

409. *Denies thee vantage.* "Will avail thee nothing" (Malone). *Wouldst* = shouldst.

419. *Confiscation.* The reading of the 2d folio ; the 1st has "confutation."

420. *Widow you.* Dower you.

423. *Definitive.* Resolved ; the only instance of the word in S. He uses *definite* once (in *Cymb.* i. 6. 43) and in the same sense.

429. *Importune.* For the accent, see on i. 1. 56 above. *Sense*=both reason and feeling (Johnson).

430. *Fact.* Deed, crime. See on iv. 2. 130 above.

447. *His act did not o'ertake his bad intent.* Steevens quotes *Macb.* iv. 1. 145 :

"The flighty purpose never is o'ertook
Unless the deed go with it."

448. *Must be buried*, etc. " Like the traveller, who dies on his journey, is obscurely interred, and thought of no more " (Steevens).

460. *After more advice.* On further consideration. Cf. *M. of V.* p. 161.

463. *What 's he?* Who is he ? See on iv. 2. 122 above.

479. *Quit.* Acquit, forgive. Cf. *A. Y. L.* p. 169.

488. *Give me your hand.* That is, if you give me your hand.

493. *Her worth worth yours.* " Her value is equal to your value, she is not unworthy of you " (Johnson). Hanmer reads " her worth works yours."

494. *Apt remission.* " Readiness to forgive " (J. H.).

495. *In place.* Present ; as in *T. of S.* i. 2. 157, 3 *Hen. VI.* iv. 1. 103, etc.

497. *Luxury.* Lust ; the only meaning in S. Cf. *Hen. V.* p. 166.

498. *Deserved so.* The folios have "so deserved ;" corrected by Pope. The Coll. MS. has "so well deserv'd."

500. *According to the trick.* According to the fashion, after the manner of young fellows.

505. *If any woman 's wrong'd.* The folio has "woman ;" corrected by Hanmer. The Camb. ed. reads, " Is any woman," etc.

508. *Nuptial.* See on iii. 1. 207 above.

517. *Pressing to death.* Alluding to the ancient punishment of the *peine forte et dure*, or pressing to death by heavy weights laid on the body. Cf. *Much Ado*, iii. 1. 76, *Rich. II.* iii. 4. 72, etc.

520. *She.* For a wonder, *not* "corrected " by Pope to *her.* See on iii. 1. 206 above.

524. *Gratulate.* To be gratulated, gratifying. For the form, see on 374 above. Hanmer reads " execute " for *executed* in 516.

534. *That 's.* The reading of the 2d folio ; the 1st has " that."

ADDENDUM.

The "Time-Analysis" of the Play.—This is summed up by Mr. P. A. Daniel, in his paper " On the Times or Durations of the Action of Shakspere's Plays " (*Trans. of New Shaks. Soc.* 1877–79, p. 139), as follows :

"The time of the Play, then, is four days :—

1. Act I. sc. i. may be taken as a kind of prelude, after which some little interval must be supposed in order to permit the new governors of the city to settle to their work. The rest of the Play is comprised in three consecutive days.

2. Commences with Act I. sc. ii. and ends in Act IV. sc. ii.

3. Commences in Act IV. sc. ii. and ends with Act IV. sc. iv.

4. Includes Act IV. sc. v. and vi. and the whole of Act V., which is in one scene only."

INDEX OF WORDS AND PHRASES
EXPLAINED.

SHAKESPEARE'S BUST.

SHAKESPEARE.

WITH NOTES BY WM. J. ROLFE, A.M.

ILLUSTRATED. 16MO, CLOTH, 56 CTS. PER VOL. ; PAPER, 40 CTS. PER VOL.

In the preparation of this edition of the English Classics it has been the aim to adapt them for school and home reading, in essentially the same way as Greek and Latin Classics are edited for educational purposes. The chief requisites are a pure text (expurgated, if necessary), and the notes needed for its thorough explanation and illustration.

Each of Shakespeare's plays is complete in one volume, and is preceded by an Introduction containing the "History of the Play," the "Sources of the Plot," and "Critical Comments on the Play."

From HORACE HOWARD FURNESS, Ph.D., LL.D., *Editor of the* "*New Variorum Shakespeare.*"

No one can examine these volumes and fail to be impressed with the conscientious accuracy and scholarly completeness with which they are edited. The educational purposes for which the notes are written Mr. Rolfe never loses sight of, but like "a well-experienced archer hits the mark his eye doth level at."

From F. J. FURNIVALL, *Director of the New Shakspere Society, London.*

The merit I see in Mr. Rolfe's school editions of Shakspere's Plays over those most widely used in England is that Mr. Rolfe edits the plays as works of a poet, and not only as productions in Tudor English. Some editors think that all they have to do with a play is to state its source and explain its hard words and allusions ; they treat it as they would a charter or a catalogue of household furniture, and then rest satisfied. But Mr. Rolfe, while clearing up all verbal difficulties as carefully as any Dryasdust, always adds the choicest extracts he can find, on the spirit and special "note" of each play, and on the leading characteristics of its chief personages. He does *not* leave the student without help in getting at Shakspere's chief attributes, his characterization and poetic power. And every practical teacher knows that while every boy can look out hard words in a lexicon for himself, not one in a score can, unhelped, catch points of and realize character, and feel and express the distinctive individuality of each play as a poetic creation.

From Prof. EDWARD DOWDEN, LL.D., *of the University of Dublin, Author of "Shakspere: His Mind and Art."*

I incline to think that no edition is likely to be so useful for school and home reading as yours. Your notes contain so much accurate instruction, with so little that is superfluous ; you do not neglect the æsthetic study of the play ; and in externals, paper, type, binding, etc., you make a book "pleasant to the eyes" (as well as "to be desired to make one wise ")—no small matter, I think, with young readers and with old.

From EDWIN A. ABBOTT, M.A., *Author of "Shakespearian Grammar."*

I have not seen any edition that compresses so much necessary information into so small a space, nor any that so completely avoids the common faults of commentaries on Shakespeare—needless repetition, superfluous explanation, and unscholar-like ignoring of difficulties.

From HIRAM CORSON, M.A., *Professor of Anglo-Saxon and English Literature, Cornell University, Ithaca, N. Y.*

In the way of annotated editions of separate plays of Shakespeare, for educational purposes, I know of none quite up to Rolfe's.

I read your "Merchant of Venice" with my class, and found it in every respect an excellent edition. I do not agree with my friend White in the opinion that Shakespeare requires but few notes—that is, if he is to be thoroughly understood. Doubtless he may be enjoyed, and many a hard place slid over. Your notes give all the help a young student requires, and yet the reader for pleasure will easily get at just what he wants. You have indeed been conscientiously concise.

Under date of July 25, 1879, Prof. CHILD *adds :* Mr. Rolfe's editions of plays of Shakespeare are very valuable and convenient books, whether for a college class or for private study. I have used them with my students, and I welcome every addition that is made to the series. They show care, research, and good judgment, and are fully up to the time in scholarship. I fully agree with the opinion that experienced teachers have expressed of the excellence of these books.

I regard your own work as of the highest merit, while you have turned the labors of others to the best possible account. I want to have the higher classes of our schools introduced to Shakespeare chief of all, and then to other standard English authors ; but this cannot be done to advantage, unless under a teacher of equally rare gifts and abundant leisure, or through editions specially prepared for such use. I trust that you will have the requisite encouragement to proceed with a work so happily begun.

We repeat what we have often said, that there is no edition of Shakespeare's which seems to us preferable to Mr. Rolfe's. As mere specimens of the printer's and binder's art they are unexcelled, and their other merits are equally high. Mr. Rolfe, having learned by the practical experience of the class-room what aid the average student really needs in order to read Shakespeare intelligently, has put just that amount of aid into his notes, and no more. Having said what needs to be said, he stops there. It is a rare virtue in the editor of a classic, and we are proportionately grateful for it.

From the N. Y. Times.

This work has been done so well that it could hardly have been done better. It shows throughout knowledge, taste, discriminating judgment, and, what is rarer and of yet higher value, a sympathetic appreciation of the poet's moods and purposes.

From the Pacific School Journal, San Francisco.

This edition of Shakespeare's plays bids fair to be the most valuable aid to the study of English literature yet published. For educational purposes it is beyond praise. Each of the plays is printed in large clear type and on excellent paper. Every difficulty of the text is clearly explained by copious notes. It is remarkable how many new beauties one may discern in Shakespeare with the aid of the glossaries attached to these books. . . . Teachers can do no higher, better work than to inculcate a love for the best literature, and such books as these will best aid them in cultivating a pure and refined taste.

From the Christian Union, N. Y.

Mr. W. J. Rolfe's capital edition of Shakespeare—by far the best edition for school and parlor use. We speak after some practical use of it in a village Shakespeare Club. The notes are brief but useful ; and the necessary expurgations are managed with discriminating skill.

From the Academy, London.

Mr. Rolfe's excellent series of school-editions of the Plays of Shakespeare. . . . Mr. Rolfe's editions differ from some of the English ones in looking on the plays as something more than word-puzzles. They give the student helps and hints on the characters and meanings of the plays, while the word-notes are also full and posted up to the latest date. . . . Mr. Rolfe also adds to each of his books a most useful " Index of Words and Phrases explained."

PUBLISHED BY HARPER & BROTHERS, NEW YORK.

Any of the above works will be sent by mail, postage prepaid, to any part of the United States, on receipt of the price.

OLIVER GOLDSMITH.

SELECT POEMS OF OLIVER GOLDSMITH. Edited, with Notes, by WILLIAM J. ROLFE, A.M., formerly Head Master of the High School, Cambridge, Mass. Illustrated. 16mo, Paper, 40 cents ; Cloth, 56 cents. (*Uniform with Rolfe's Shakespeare.*)

The carefully arranged editions of "The Merchant of Venice" and other of Shakespeare's plays prepared by Mr. William J. Rolfe for the use of students will be remembered with pleasure by many readers, and they will welcome another volume of a similar character from the same source, in the form of the "Select Poems of Oliver Goldsmith," edited with notes fuller than those of any other known edition, many of them original with the editor.—*Boston Transcript.*

Mr. Rolfe is doing very useful work in the preparation of compact hand-books for study in English literature. His own personal culture, and his long experience as a teacher, give him good knowledge of what is wanted in this way.—*The Congregationalist*, Boston.

Mr. Rolfe has prefixed to the Poems selections illustrative of Goldsmith's character as a man and grade as a poet, from sketches by Macaulay, Thackeray, George Colman, Thomas Campbell, John Forster, and Washington Irving. He has also appended, at the end of the volume, a body of scholarly notes explaining and illustrating the poems, and dealing with the times in which they were written, as well as the incidents and circumstances attending their composition. — *Christian Intelligencer*, N. Y.

The notes are just and discriminating in tone, and supply all that is necessary either for understanding the thought of the several poems, or for a critical study of the language. The use of such books in the school-room cannot but contribute largely toward putting the study of English literature upon a sound basis ; and many an adult reader would find in the present volume an excellent opportunity for becoming critically acquainted with one of the greatest of last century's poets.—*Appleton's Journal*, N. Y.

PUBLISHED BY HARPER & BROTHERS, NEW YORK.

☞ *Sent by mail, postage prepaid, to any part of the United States, on receipt of the price.*

THOMAS GRAY.

SELECT POEMS OF THOMAS GRAY. Edited, with
Notes, by WILLIAM J. ROLFE, A.M., formerly Head
Master of the High School, Cambridge, Mass. Illus-
trated. Square 16mo, Paper, 40 cents ; Cloth, 56 cents.
(*Uniform with Rolfe's Shakespeare.*)

Mr. Rolfe has done his work in a manner that comes as near to perfection as man can approach. He knows his subject so well that he is
competent to instruct all in it ; and readers will find an immense amount
of knowledge in his elegant volume, all set forth in the most admirable
order, and breathing the most liberal and enlightened spirit, he being a
warm appreciator of the divinity of genius.—*Boston Traveller.*

The great merit of these books lies in their carefully-edited text, and in
the fulness of their explanatory notes. Mr. Rolfe is not satisfied with
simply expounding, but he explores the entire field of English literature,
and therefrom gathers a multitude of illustrations that are interesting in
themselves and valuable as a commentary on the text. He not only in-
structs, but stimulates his readers to fresh exertion ; and it is this stimu-
lation that makes his labors so productive in the school-room.—*Saturday
Evening Gazette*, Boston.

Mr. William J. Rolfe, to whom English literature is largely indebted
for annotated and richly-illustrated editions of several of Shakespeare's
Plays, has treated the "Select Poems of Thomas Gray" in the same way
—just as he had previously dealt with the best of Goldsmith's poems.—
The Press, Phila.

Mr. Rolfe's edition of Thomas Gray's select poems is marked by the
same discriminating taste as his other classics.—*Springfield Republican.*

Mr. Rolfe's rare abilities as a teacher and his fine scholarly tastes enable him to prepare a classic like this in the best manner for school use.
There could be no better exercise for the advanced classes in our schools
than the critical study of our best authors, and the volumes that Mr. Rolfe
has prepared will hasten the time when the study of mere form will give
place to the study of the spirit of our literature.—*Louisville Courier-
Journal.*

An elegant and scholarly little volume.—*Christian Intelligencer*, N. Y.

PUBLISHED BY HARPER & BROTHERS, NEW YORK.

☞ *Sent by mail, postage prepaid, to any part of the United States, on receipt of the
price and one sixth additional for postage.*